# THE DISCOVERY COLLECTION

## THE DISCOVERY COLLECTION

*The Discovery*
*Ambush at Cisco Swamp*
*Armoured Defence*
*The Dinosaur Feather*


## THE WILDERNESS COLLECTION

*Call of the Wild*
*Dino Champions*
*Dinosaur Cove*
*Eruption!*

# THE DISCOVERY COLLECTION

RANDOM HOUSE AUSTRALIA

A Random House book
Published by Random House Australia Pty Ltd
Level 3, 100 Pacific Highway, North Sydney NSW 2060
www.randomhouse.com.au

*Robert Irwin, Dinosaur Hunter 1: The Discovery* first published by
Random House Australia in 2013
*Robert Irwin, Dinosaur Hunter 2: Ambush at Cisco Swamp* first
published by Random House Australia in 2013
*Robert Irwin, Dinosaur Hunter 3: Armoured Defence* first published
by Random House Australia in 2013
*Robert Irwin, Dinosaur Hunter 4: The Dinosaur Feather* first
published by Random House Australia in 2013
This omnibus edition first published by Random House Australia
in 2014

The publisher would like to thank David Elliott from the Australian
Age of Dinosaurs.

Addresses for companies within the Random House Group can be
found at www.randomhouse.com.au/offices

National Library of Australia
Cataloguing-in-Publication Entry

Author: Irwin, Robert, 2003–
Title: Robert Irwin, Dinosaur Hunter 1–4: The Discovery Collection/
Robert Irwin, Jack Wells.
ISBN: 978 0 85798 511 8 (pbk)
Series: Robert Irwin; 1–4.
Target Audience: For primary school age.
Subjects: Dinosaurs – Juvenile fiction.
Other Authors/Contributors: Kunz, Chris; Kelly, Helen; Harding, David.
Dewey Number: A823.4

Illustrations by Lachlan Creagh
Cover and internal design by Christabella Designs
Typeset by Midland Typesetters, Australia
Printed in Australia by Griffin Press, an accredited ISO AS/NZS
14001:2004 Environmental Management System printer

Random House Australia uses papers that are natural, renewable and
recyclable products and made from wood grown in sustainable forests.
The logging and manufacturing processes are expected to conform to
the environmental regulations of the country of origin.

# THE DISCOVERY

## WRITTEN BY JACK WELLS

RANDOM HOUSE AUSTRALIA

# CHAPTER ONE

The assassin focused in on his target. It was going to be easy. The target was concentrating so hard, there was no way he'd notice the stealthy footfalls of the assassin as he came at the target from behind. It was going to be the easiest job the assassin had had in ages. So easy, in

fact, he wondered if he should delay it until the target could at least put up a bit of a fight.

Nah, he'd destroy him now anyway.

Then he could go dirt bike riding.

The assassin crept closer and closer. The dinosaur mask he was wearing was getting hot, and the eyeholes kept moving. He could only hope the target was still in sight. He couldn't actually tell for sure. The target was using a handheld power tool, so there would be no way of hearing the assassin move with the stealth of a tiger and

the weightlessness of something really light – maybe a feather – yeah, a feather. The target would be mincemeat and not even know how he got minced, this assassin was that good.

Two more footsteps and the target would be done, good and proper . . .

Unexpectedly, the target turned around, brandishing what looked like a dentist's drill, and shouted 'Riiiiiiiillley!' really loud.

Riley the assassin jumped a mile into the air in fright.

His best friend Robert, aka the target,

howled with laughter. 'Awesome mask. Is it meant to be an *allosaurus*?'

Riley ripped off the mask. 'I don't know. I just picked it up at the museum shop. I thought I'd actually scare you this time.'

Robert smirked. 'Good luck with that, mate.'

'But I was sure I'd got you. You were so busy looking at that boring old rock.'

Robert was shocked. 'This is no boring old rock! This is the most exciting rock *ever*.'

Riley raised an eyebrow.

'C'mon, mate, you know what's inside this rock, don't you?'

'A whole lot of smaller rocks squashed together?' said Riley, playing dumb.

'Nup,' answered Robert. 'Inside this rock is a dinosaur fossil, which is what makes this rock so awesome. Didn't you listen when we went out with the palaeontologist this morning?'

'Kind of. Well, not really. Out the window I could see some excellent trails that would be good for dirt-biking.'

Robert was still holding the rock. He hadn't finished trying to convince

his friend of how amazing fossils were. 'Once upon a time, this fossil was a part of a real-life dinosaur that roamed prehistoric Australia. It might have been a huge carnivore the size of four elephants or a scrawny feathered herbivore the size of an oversized rooster. That's what I want to find out.'

Riley was still not convinced. 'Who cares? They lived ages ago.'

Robert grinned. 'Exactly. That's what makes it so exciting!'

'Speaking of exciting, wanna go

dirt bike riding?' asked his best friend, completely missing the point.

'Later. I just want to spend a bit more time with this guy,' said Robert, looking fondly at the rock in his hand. 'But if you find the best tracks, you can count on a race later on.'

Riley gave his mate a friendly whack on the back of the head with the dinosaur mask. 'You bet. And then you'll really be scared. Scared of my speed and skill!'

Robert smiled as Riley trudged out the door of the dinosaur fossil laboratory and into the glaring Queensland sunshine.

He turned to an impressive-looking figure in the corner of the lab – a large fossil of the leg of a titanosaur, which had been affectionately named Wade. The poor 'saur was currently missing a head, a tail and quite a few bits in-between, but the size of its leg made it clear that, once upon a time, this enormous dinosaur was probably the size of a small building!

'Wade, not everyone loves dinosaurs the way I do. I don't understand it, but I have to accept it. Now, if you're lucky, in this rock I might just uncover another

piece of you. That'd be good, wouldn't it?
I know you'd like to be more than just a
large leg. Let's see if I can help you with
that.'

Robert turned on the drill, which was
actually called an air scribe, a specialised
tool used to help remove rock from
around fossils, and once again focused
on his special task.

For Robert Irwin, life didn't get much
better than this. Here he was in a dino
laboratory in outback Australia, helping
to uncover new fossils at the Australian
Age of Dinosaurs – best birthday present
ever!

# CHAPTER TWO

A few weeks before Robert's ninth birthday, his mum had asked what he'd like most in the world. He didn't hesitate. He knew *exactly* what he wanted.

Robert lived with his mum and his sister, Bindi, at Australia Zoo, on Queensland's Sunshine Coast. It was a

fantastic place for a boy to grow up. He already knew he was one of the luckiest kids in the world, and although he really, really loved lots of living creatures, what Robert loved even more were creatures that had roamed the earth a long time ago: creatures with enormous tails and enormous teeth, creatures that ruled the world long before humans were around.

Dinosaurs.

Big ones, small ones, feathered ones, flying ones. It didn't matter. He loved them all.

After some serious organisation involving new tyres for the Land Cruiser, camping gear and a new bike rack for their dirt bikes, the Irwins, along with Robert's best friend, Riley, drove northwest for hours, away from the Queensland coast. Finally, they arrived at a small outback town called Winton, a place where some very exciting dinosaur discoveries had recently been made. It was also home to Australia's only museum dedicated to Australian dinosaurs.

Even after hours of driving, Robert was nowhere near running out of

dinosaur facts. '... And in 1964 they discovered *Minmi paravertebra* (min-mee par-ah-ver-te-bra), an ankylosaur, a four-legged dinosaur with body armour. *Minmi* was the first ankylosaur found in the Southern Hemisphere.'

Riley looked over at his friend. 'How do you remember all this stuff?'

Robert shrugged. 'I just do. He was a cute little dino that lived in the early Cretaceous period, and was only about a metre tall.'

'So he wouldn't have eaten me?' asked Riley.

'No, I think he was a plant-eater. And judging by the fact that he was covered in armour, *minmi* looks like he was built to defend himself rather than attack others. Those armoured plates are called scutes, just like what crocs have.'

Robert knew a lot about crocodiles, because he was the son of the famous Crocodile Hunter, Steve Irwin, who had devoted his life to caring for animals, especially crocodiles, before his untimely death when Robert was still small. Apart from looking just like his dad, Robert also shared his adventurous spirit.

After their first night camping, Robert and Riley were up early the next morning to go out on a dig with a palaeontologist called Paul Battersby and a few other volunteers from the Queensland Museum. The dig site was about 40 kilometres outside Winton on a large sheep station. The area had already produced some important fossil finds and had been prepared, waiting for the small group to begin work. Robert was bursting with excitement!

They had brought a range of tools with them, from geo picks, rock hammers and

chisels, to a range of different brushes. This was hard, hot and exacting work, and you needed a lot of patience and concentration to work under these conditions. It was unusual for a 9-year-old to be allowed to dig in the first place, but Robert Irwin wasn't your normal 9-year-old. He had started writing letters to palaeontologists around the time other kids became interested in writing to Santa.

On the other hand, it didn't take Riley long to lose interest. He went off in search of termite mounds. 'Riley, mate, don't go

upsetting any more of the wildlife,' said Robert with a grin.

A day earlier, the two of them had found a meat ant nest near their camp site. Riley couldn't resist poking a stick into the nest, only to regret his decision seconds later as an army of ants ran up his stick and attacked. The angry red bites were still itching all up Riley's right arm.

'Yep, I know. Looking, not touching,' replied Riley with a serious nod. He wasn't going to inflict that kind of pain on himself again any time soon.

As the small group began to fossick around the area, they could feel the curious eyes of a few sheep in a nearby paddock. Humans did a whole lot of strange things, but the sheep could not make head nor woolly tail of what this group was up to!

For the first half hour, the group combed the area, occasionally stopping to dig if something caught their eye.

'I'm just going to check out this area over here,' Robert called out as he took a swig of water from his drink bottle. The sun was shining bright when his eye

caught sight of something. He wandered closer to an interesting clump of grass, and found an unusually shaped rock.

Could it be?

'Paul, come over here!' Robert tried to contain his excitement.

Paul was a veteran when it came to these digs. He'd been taking part in dinosaur discoveries for over 20 years, all over the world. With his sun-bleached blond hair and warm smile, he was a palaeontologist who never got tired of the excitement of a potential find. He strolled over and took a close look at the rock. 'I'm sorry, little guy,' he said, patting Robert on the back. 'Not this time.'

Robert grinned, undiscouraged. 'No worries.' And he immediately went back to scouring the ground once more.

Paul took off his hat and admired the boy's determination. 'You're a true-blue dinosaur hunter, you know that?'

Robert chuckled, not taking his eyes off the ground in front of him as he continued to scan the area. 'Yeah, just like my dad was the Crocodile Hunter, I'll be Robert Irwin the Dinosaur Hunter.'

'It definitely has a ring to it,' said Paul, with a chuckle.

Bailey, a volunteer, added, 'All you need to make it come true is to –'

'Hey, take a look at this!' With his geo pick, Robert dug carefully around what looked to be a partially buried boulder.

'– find a dinosaur,' Bailey finished with a grin.

Paul bent down to take a closer look at what Robert had unearthed. 'Ah, now *this* could be something special.'

Robert continued to carefully remove

the soil around the boulder. His geo pick tapped against something only a couple of centimetres away from a bigger boulder. Paul was smiling. 'Just dig really carefully around there . . . Looks like it might be . . .'

Robert changed from the pick to a largish brush, and carefully swept away the loose soil. 'A dinosaur claw?!'

Paul grinned. 'Yeah, I think you're right, Robert. Looks like it might be a claw. As well as some kind of much bigger fossil inside the boulder right next to it.'

Robert, wearing a grin the size of a crocodile's, stood up and raised both hands in the air like he'd just won an Olympic gold medal. 'I found a fossil. *Two* fossils. Doubly awesome!'

# CHAPTER THREE

Robert's moment of triumph was interrupted by Riley limping back to the dig site, holding one of his feet and yelping in pain.

Robert rushed over to his friend in concern. 'What is it? A snake bite? Another meat ant attack?'

Riley shook his head. 'Nope.' He looked a little bashful. 'A bee sting.'

While one of the volunteers went off in search of the first aid kit, Robert sat with his friend at the edge of the dig site.

'We'll have to give you a new nickname, mate. Riley the Insect Aggravator,' suggested Robert with a straight face.

'I don't like that nickname.' Riley glared at his best friend before returning to watch his bee sting grow red and swell.

Robert thought it might be a good idea to change the subject. Perhaps now wasn't the time to pay out his friend,

who was obviously in pain. 'Well, I've got a new nickname – it's Robert Irwin the Dinosaur Hunter. And I've just found dino fossils.'

Riley brightened at the news. 'That's awesome! What dinosaur do they belong to?'

Robert shrugged. 'I don't know yet. It actually takes months, sometimes even years, to work out which creature a fossil belongs to. It's like a massive jigsaw puzzle where you first have to work out which pieces belong to what puzzle.'

Riley yawned. He didn't have the

patience for jigsaw puzzles. 'Robert Irwin the Dinosaur Hunter's a beaut nickname.' He started feeling sorry for himself. 'I want a nickname like that.'

'How about Riley the Dirt Bike Champion?' suggested Robert, trying to make his friend feel better.

Riley smiled, warming to the idea immediately. 'Yeah, that'll do.'

Back at the lab, Robert was getting peckish. It was feeling like afternoon-snack time. He took out his digital voice

recorder and made a quick update.

'1600 hours on 10 March 2013. Lab work. After three hours using the air scribe, I've managed to uncover another five centimetres of fossil. I reckon I might be working on a femur, which is a thigh bone.' Robert turned to Wade in the corner. 'Sorry, Wade, I don't think you're going to get more body parts out of me today.'

Robert admitted to himself that it was frustrating it would take so long before the fossil he'd found this morning could be linked to an actual

dinosaur. He couldn't stop thinking about the claw. Imagine if it was from his favourite dinosaur, *Australovenator wintonensis* (oss-tra-low-ven-ah-tor win-ton-en-sis)! But he wouldn't know for months, maybe even years.

He finished his update and slipped the recorder back into his jacket. For the past year, Robert had been recording all of his dinosaur adventures on his digital voice recorder, and was planning on putting together a journal of all his discoveries.

'Owww!' As he got up from his chair, Robert felt a sharp prod from the back

pocket of his shorts. He looked around. The lab was empty. Even before he could reach into his back pocket there was another sharp prod. 'Owww! What is *that*?' He reached into his shorts pocket and pulled out . . . a fossilised claw!

'Hang on, where did this come from?' He looked closely at the fossil. 'It could be the claw I found on the dig this morning. But how . . .?'

Once the claw had been carefully dug up, Robert had given the fossil to Paul, and it had been wrapped and loaded onto a truck with the other fossils found that day. Robert couldn't think of an explanation as to how it came to be in his back pocket.

He looked around at the deserted lab, and started to feel a bit dizzy. The walls of the laboratory looked like they were bending inwards, and the ground below him began to shimmer. He took hold of the fossil in both hands and, suddenly, the dizziness became a lot more intense, like he was getting dragged down a plughole really fast.

Robert managed to call out a weak 'Rillleeeeey . . .' before he blacked out.

# CHAPTER FOUR

Robert rolled over and groaned. Since when was his bed this uncomfortable? It was definitely time for a new pillow. This one was hard and cold, and eeugh, was that moss tickling his nose? *Gross*. He slowly opened one eye, then the other, and surveyed his surroundings.

No, he wasn't in bed and this certainly wasn't his pillow. He got up from the mossy rock he'd been leaning on. It was deathly quiet. He was in a forested area – bushland somewhere – but he had no idea where.

Robert tried to remember how he'd got here. But nothing came to mind. How *had* he got here?

'Riley? Mum, are you here?' he called out groggily.

A slight wind whistled through the trees. Robert got the feeling there wasn't a single human being around for miles.

He shivered, wrapping his jacket around him for warmth.

Maybe he was dreaming. He vaguely remembered being in the fossil lab with Riley trying to sneak up on him. He wasn't even tired. Why would he have fallen asleep?

He looked around and found the fossilised claw lying next to the mossy rock. Without quite knowing why, he reached over gingerly and touched it with both hands. Nothing happened.

None of this made any sense at all.

All of a sudden the ground started to vibrate. Robert looked up in alarm. Where was he and what was happening? Was this an earthquake? Or an erupting volcano? He couldn't see a volcano from where he was but, right now, he wasn't about to rule anything out. It didn't feel like any dream he'd ever had before. This was far too real!

The trees and ferns around him were pulsing in time with the vibrations, and there was a sound, a sort of a dull thrum, which was building second by second.

Robert's intuition told him to get off the ground – and fast. He shoved the fossil back into his pocket to think about later, then raced to the nearest tree and started to climb.

Once he was a few metres above the ground, Robert stopped and settled himself onto a branch. The vibrations became more intense, and in the distance he could see a large dust cloud moving rapidly in his direction.

Robert had heard of the massive migrations that animals like wildebeest and antelope made every year in Africa, but he'd never seen one firsthand. Could he be in Africa?

His hands shook as got out his voice recorder. Whatever it was he was about to see, he wanted to make sure it was documented.

He checked his watch and saw the battery was dead. He must have bumped it when he blacked out. He pressed record on his digital voice recorder. 'Ummm, not sure how to start this entry. I'm somewhere, I don't know exactly where . . . I'm up a tree, watching a large dust cloud move closer and closer. The

ground below me is shaking, and I have absolutely no idea what's coming my way.'

Robert held his breath. For now, there was nothing else to say.

# CHAPTER FIVE

The sound of thunderous galloping was overwhelming. The dust was making it hard to see but it looked like a herd of...

Robert wiped the dust from his eyes and peered down into the cloud.

43

He almost fell out of the tree. Dinosaurs?!

He felt the fossil in his back pocket. 'I've travelled back in time?' This was impossible. Was someone going to come out from behind a tree and say 'Just kidding!'?

The herd was galloping past, along the dusty path below Robert's tree. They were fast, bird-like dinosaurs that ran on two legs. Real-life dinosaurs! Robert's brain churned through all the dinosaur info he had stored in his head. He thought they could be ornithopods. If he was right, they were herbivorous, which meant they were plant-eaters and posed no direct threat to him. Although, if he'd stayed on the ground, it wouldn't have been so comfortable getting stepped on by stampeding dinosaurs, even if they were small ones!

Once the dust cloud cleared, Robert coughed a little and took a few seconds to rub the dirt from his eyes, trying to remain quiet. He wasn't sure if the ornithopods were being chased or whether they were just travelling to a new location.

When the last one disappeared from sight, Robert waited until he was sure no predator was following the herd, then he climbed down from the tree and onto the dusty track.

Okay, so he had travelled back in time. This wasn't a dream or a practical joke. And it had to have something to do with the fossil he'd found. Even though he still felt dazed by the discovery, Robert realised that this was the chance of a lifetime. He wasn't going to waste time thinking about it. He had things to check out! Robert started jogging along

the path left by the ornithopod herd, excitement building in his chest.

As he ran, he recorded an update. 'Can you believe it? I reckon that somehow I've ended up in prehistoric Australia, possibly some time in the Cretaceous period. It's incredible. I've just seen my first herd of dinosaurs. I think the group were ornithopods, which are about the size of emus. They're herbivores, they walk on two legs and travel in packs.'

Robert looked around as the landscape began to change. He was leaving the forest behind and could see that a clearing lay ahead. Travelling a few steps further, he paused when he found the pack had stopped to drink from a muddy riverbank. He crouched down, lowering his voice to a whisper.

'Within the group, it looks like there are both adults and juveniles. The river they're drinking from is probably familiar to them, as they seemed to know the direction they were heading in. And they're not the only species using the river as a watering hole. I'm going to take a closer look.'

Robert snuck as close as he thought was safe, his shoes sinking slightly into the muddy soil. 'Crikey, I think the other dinosaurs may be coelurosaurs. Amazing creatures! They're brown and leathery with long necks and small beady eyes. They're known to be carnivorous, which means they're meat-eaters, but they don't seem interested in taking a bite out of the ornithopods. They're a smaller species. In fact – take a look at that – I can see a few of the coelurosaurs snapping at insects near the water's edge. Smaller food items, like frogs or small reptiles, are probably more within their reach.'

Robert stopped recording and took a deep breath. What had started off as a really good birthday present – a dinosaur dig and fossil preparation – had just become a million times better! This present had become totally out of this world! If only Riley could see it as well – then he'd understand how awesome dinosaurs really were!

When Robert could bear to tear his eyes away from the dinosaurs, he took a closer look at the surrounding

environment. It was a much cooler climate here than it had been in the hot sun of present-day Winton. He was lucky he'd kept his jacket on while he'd been in the lab. And there were no gum trees or grass here now. He knew that cycads, gingko trees and various different types of fern were a part of Australia in the Cretaceous period, but to see them with his own eyes was just incredible!

All of a sudden, an enormous roar ripped through the air. Robert stifled a yelp and sprinted as fast as he could into the relative safety of the bushland. He hid, shaking, behind a small tree fern at the edge of the clearing.

His heart was pounding.

Of course, it was fine to get excited about living in the time of dinosaurs, but the tricky thing was working out how to stay alive when there were so many enormous, meat-eating giants roaming the place!

# CHAPTER SIX

Robert wasn't the only one alarmed by the terrifying sound. The herd of dinosaurs drinking by the stream panicked. They stampeded in all directions, causing mayhem, squealing and braying as they tried to gallop out of harm's way.

Despite his fear, Robert knew he had to get a look at the creature that could produce a roar like that. He inched his way to a position, still half-hidden by fern fronds, where he could watch the drama unfold.

And then the beast appeared. On two legs, scaly and terrifying, the creature let out another bellow. His gleaming rows of razor-like teeth were making it clear to the smaller dinosaurs that they were most definitely on the menu! Robert couldn't believe his luck. He had to remind himself to breathe. 'I think this

guy . . . this guy is an *australovenator*.
It's incredible to see him in the flesh.
He's called the Southern Hunter and he's
absolutely fearsome. He's a carnivore.
And I reckon it's just about lunchtime.
There's no doubt about it. The smaller
dinos know this and are running for their
lives.'

The *australovenator* ran towards
the group of smaller dinosaurs, causing
them to scramble, some sprinting away
from the creature and, strangely, some
running straight towards it. It was like
watching an unusual prehistoric game

of chicken. The small 'saurs were much quicker than the hungry theropod, but the size of his claws made Robert believe the *australovenator* would not leave the river's edge with an empty stomach!

# CHAPTER SEVEN

The stampede was over in moments. The *australovenator* was able to grab hold of a coelurosaur that had become trapped on the mudflats and, with a swipe of his claws, the smaller dinosaur was dead. And seconds after that, it had been eaten. This carnivore wasted

no time on good table manners.

Robert pressed record and whispered, 'This is just the first course for a dinosaur of this size. I'd better make sure I don't move a muscle until he's well on his way to finding his next course! Hopefully his dessert is waiting for him a couple of kilometres away.'

None of the coelurosaurs or ornithopods had hung around to watch the quick feast. The dinosaur shook his head and bellowed. 'Did I just hear a dinosaur burp?' wondered Robert, and watched as the beast slowly loped down to the edge of the riverbank and back the way he had come.

Robert realised his heart was still thumping in his chest. The creature was terrifying ... and incredible! He waited until his heartbeat had returned to normal and his hands had stopped shaking, then he waited a few more minutes to make sure the theropod was long gone before deciding to emerge from his hiding place.

Taking a deep breath, Robert looked around. His legs were still a bit shaky. It was now eerily quiet. All that remained were hundreds of dinosaur tracks in the mud. Robert walked down to the water's edge and pressed record once more on his voice recorder.

'Although it's incredible to be here, I'm starting to wonder just how or if I can get back to my life in 2013.' He felt scared and alone. Surviving in this harsh environment would be really hard, maybe even impossible. Where could he find a place to stay safe and uneaten? What would he eat? He imagined grabbing hold of vines and swinging through the forest like Tarzan, trying to escape the

claws of countless terrifying creatures. If he could find a *minmi*, he could maybe make friends with it. They could set up camp together. And chances are it wouldn't be as accident prone as Riley. But it probably wouldn't crack jokes either. Robert grimaced. If he was stuck here, it would be hard . . . and lonely. He swallowed the lump that had formed in his throat.

'You'll be all right, mate,' he said to himself, trying to cheer himself up. 'Who knows what might happen to Riley if I'm not there to save him from his next insect attack?' Pulling the fossilised claw from his back pocket, Robert stared at it for a moment. 'How do I get back home?' he asked in a quiet voice. He waited a few moments but the fossil didn't answer. He sighed.

And behind him, he heard another sigh, which was more like a snort. Turning around slowly, Robert found himself staring into the face of another *australovenator*, a smaller version of the earlier scary one. Although, admittedly, this one was still pretty scary!

It had leant down to give Robert a

sniff. This was the first time it had come across a creature like this!

For a dinosaur that might have weighed around 350 kilograms, he was surprisingly light on his feet. Robert hadn't heard a thing.

His heart thumped hard against his rib cage. He was too scared to breathe. On the one hand, Robert was thrilled – his favourite dinosaur was so close he could touch him.

Robert's scientific brain, even under this much stress, couldn't help cataloguing the amazing specimen in front of him:

the long claws and its razor-sharp teeth. It was a mottled colour. Brown and a little reddish. The claws looked strikingly similar to the fossilised one Robert held in his hand. He was pretty sure he no longer needed to wait for confirmation that he'd discovered an *australovenator* claw back in modern-day Australia – the proof was right here in front of him. The 'proof' also had really bad breath. Now *that* was something that was never mentioned in dinosaur museums!

On the other hand, the *australove-nator* was called the Southern Hunter for

a good reason. This was a bloodthirsty carnivorous dinosaur, and even though this one was young, Robert couldn't help thinking that he just might get to feel the strength of the dino's jaws firsthand . . . any second now.

Luckily, it seemed that Robert was not a food source the young theropod was familiar with, and the dinosaur was still hesitating.

Robert didn't know what to do. Instinct told him he shouldn't run. Instead, he raised the fossilised claw. 'Look, mate,' he spoke in a husky voice.

'Do you reckon this claw could've belonged to you or one of your family?'

The *australovenator* leant even closer to Robert's face. Robert tried not to offend the dinosaur by screwing up his nose but he couldn't help thinking, 'Man, if I had a mint, I'd offer it. This guy has seriously not brushed his teeth for a century!' Luckily, the dino couldn't mind-read.

The *australovenator* glared at Robert for a second longer, took a sniff of the fossil, stood up to his full towering height and let out an almighty roar.

# CHAPTER EIGHT

The force of the noise hurled Robert, who was still clutching the fossilised claw, into the lapping water of the river's edge. It was cold! He struggled to find his footing on the muddy bank but was then overwhelmed by a wave of dizziness. What was happening now? Taking a

deep breath, Robert blinked his eyes in an attempt to focus them. The dizziness increased. The *australovenator* turned to take one last look at Robert before roaring once more and bounding off in the same direction the larger dinosaur had gone.

After what felt like seconds later but was in actual fact millennia later, Robert opened his eyes and found himself back in the laboratory. He was soaking wet, and holding on tightly to the fossil. The lab was empty, although he could hear Riley calling him from outside.

'Robert, I've eaten six scones already and I'll take the last three if you don't come and get 'em in the next 10 seconds. 10 . . . 9 . . . 8 . . . 7 . . . 6 . . .'

It was so good to hear his friend's voice. Robert blinked and checked he had two arms, two legs and his head was still on top of his neck.

His stomach rumbled. A scone or three sounded good. Dinosaur hunting built up an appetite, that was for sure!

Robert stood up, feeling dazed but exhilarated. He had no explanation of how it had happened, or why it had happened, but he knew it really had happened.

This was no strange dream or hallucination. The fossil he was holding was special, and it had chosen him. And it had helped answer Robert's question about who the dinosaur claw had belonged to. This was a magic fossil and he knew he'd have to keep it safe.

'You'd better leave me some scones,

Riley, or there'll be trouble,' Robert shouted, wondering how he was going to explain how he'd come to be so wet. 'I'm starving!'

# CHAPTER NINE

The next day the Irwin family and Riley travelled south of Winton to a place called Lark Quarry Conservation Park.

Today they were taking a tour around the largest recorded dinosaur stampede in the world. This was the last day of the Robert Irwin Birthday Spectacular, and

Robert was still buzzing from yesterday's birthday surprise! He still wasn't quite sure what this now meant for him. Would it happen again? Did he have any control over where or when he would travel back in time? It was thrilling but also pretty scary at the same time.

To explain away his wet clothing, Robert had made a lame joke about dodgy bathroom plumbing when he met up with Riley and his family outside the laboratory and, bizarrely, they had believed him.

The tour group moved on to another

part of the exhibit as the guide explained that palaeontologists had worked out that a large theropod had appeared by the river's edge, frightening a group of ornithopods and coelurosaurs, causing the stampede to occur.

And because it had rained a few days after the event, the water from the river had risen and covered the dino tracks with a sandy sediment, preserving the dramatic event of millions of years ago.

It all sounded very, very familiar to Robert.

Riley was impressed. 'I think I'm starting to see why you like dinosaurs so much, Robert. It's pretty sweet that these guys can tell what happened just by looking at some old tracks. And from such a long time ago. Imagine what it would've been like back then!'

Robert turned to his friend. 'Those guys were really scared, you know. The *australovenator* was terrifying.'

Riley gave him a quizzical look. 'Hang on, the guide didn't say anything about it being an austrowhatsisname. I think he just called it a theropod.'

'Oh, right. Well, I reckon it *could've* been an *australovenator*.'

Riley nodded. 'Knowing you and the stuff you read about dinosaurs all the time instead of dirt-biking with me, you're probably right.'

'Yeah, maybe.' Robert looked back at the hundreds of track marks in the display.

The reassuring prod that came from his back pocket made it clear that keeping his new discovery a secret was the right thing to do.

For now.

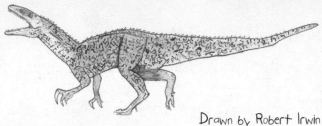

Drawn by Robert Irwin

# AUSTRALOVENATOR

SCIENTIFIC NAME: *Australovenator wintonensis*

DISCOVERED: June 2006 in the Winton

Formation, central western

Queensland

ETYMOLOGY: Winton's Southern Hunter

PERIOD: Mid-Cretaceous, 100-98 million

years ago

LENGTH: Approximately 5 metres long

HEIGHT: Approximately 1.5 metres

tall at the hip

WEIGHT: Approximately 500 kilograms

Nicknamed 'Banjo' after the Australian poet Banjo Paterson, *Australovenator* is Australia's most complete skeleton of a carnivorous (meat-eating) dinosaur. Among the fossils discovered are nine teeth, both lower jaws, some ribs and bones belonging to the dinosaur's forearms, thigh, shins and feet.

Judging from its dimensions, *australovenator* was built for speed. Palaeontologists also found finger and wrist bones along with a middle claw that revealed hands close to 50 centimetres long that could spread to a whopping 30 centimetres wide at the tip of its claws! This means that Banjo would have had a massive grasping capability.

By scanning the fossils and then creating a mirror image of them through the use of 3D-imaging technology, experts were able to create an image of two complete forearms, which can be used to work out exactly how *australovenator* attacked its prey. It is believed that *australovenator* would have dug its mighty claws into its prey, holding it in an iron grip, before going in for the kill.

## PREHISTORIC AUSTRALIA

When dinosaurs roamed the earth, Australia was part of the supercontinent, Gondwana. It was made up of most of the landmasses in today's Southern

Hemisphere, including Australia, Antarctica, Africa, South America and India.

Most of the dinosaur fossils found in Australia belong to the Cretaceous period (146-65 million years ago). During this time the Australian part of Gondwana was close to the South Pole. Australia had a temperate and humid climate, and for several weeks of each year, southern parts of Australia, such as Victoria, may have had an icy polar winter that included semi-darkness.

Towering conifer forests covered much of Australia during the Cretaceous period, and there were also smaller plants such as ferns, gingkoes, cycads, clubmosses and horsetails. This period of Australia's history also saw the appearance of the first flowering plants.

Most Australian dinosaurs have been found in the eastern half of Australia (Queensland, New South Wales and Victoria), though isolated dinosaur bones have also been unearthed in Western Australia and South Australia. Queensland, in particular, is a dinosaur hotspot, with two-thirds of the state being covered by Cretaceous rock.

# THE AUSTRALIAN AGE OF DINOSAURS MUSEUM OF NATURAL HISTORY

Australian Age of Dinosaurs Inc. was formed in Winton, Queensland in August 2002.

Since then they have organised annual dinosaur digs in western Queensland, primarily in collaboration with the Queensland Museum. This has led to the discovery and recovery of what is now the world's largest collection of Australian dinosaur fossils.

In July 2006, they opened a fossil preparation facility, and in 2009 they announced to the world the discovery of three new species of Australian dinosaurs.

Banjo (carnivorous theropod) and Matilda and Clancy (giant plant-eating sauropods) were found in a vast geological deposit near Winton that dates from 98-95 million years ago.

The meat-eating *Australovenator wintonensis* (Banjo) has been coined Australia's answer to *Velociraptor*.

Palaeontologists say that *Diamantinasaurus matildae* (Matilda) was a solid and robust animal, filling a niche similar to the hippopotamus today.

The second new species, *Wintonotitan wattsi* (Clancy) represented a tall animal that may have been Australia's prehistoric answer to the giraffe.

New fossil beds are discovered each year in the Winton Formation, proving that there has never been a more etciting time for Australian palaeontology.

# ROBERT IRWIN
## DINOSAUR HUNTER

# AMBUSH AT CISCO SWAMP
## WRITTEN BY JACK WELLS

RANDOM HOUSE AUSTRALIA

# CHAPTER ONE

'Hey Robert! Catch!' yelled Riley with a big grin on his face.

Robert instinctively threw his hands up in preparation, dropped them quickly and then jumped out of the way. He knew Riley could not be trusted at all when he was smiling like that. He turned round

just in time to see the missile land in the water behind him.

'Oh, Riley, that is too gross, even for you! Alligator poo! Eww . . .' said Robert.

'Riley! Robert!' came a loud and familiar voice. Both boys looked guiltily at each other and then in the direction of Riley's dad, who was approaching along the edge of the swamp. He didn't seem happy.

'One more scrap of mischief from you two and you'll find yourselves back at camp, peeling potatoes for the afternoon!' he said, eyeing each of them in turn. 'This is no place for silliness, not with all this going on. Everyone's busy, and if you're going to help you need to keep your wits about you at all times! Understood? This is your final warning.'

Both boys looked suitably sorry. They muttered their apologies and together breathed a sigh of relief as Scott Harper walked back the way he had come.

'That was your fault!' said Riley, elbowing Robert in the tummy until they were both laughing again. 'You should have just caught it!'

Although the boys were supposed to be helping, the exciting work was too dangerous for them to really do anything other than watch and keep a safe distance away. The day was hot and they were getting bored and restless.

The boys had been looking forward to this trip all summer and now here they were, on day three of the research trip to the Cisco Swamp in Texas, the second biggest state in the USA. The annual population survey of American alligators was in full swing and the team of reptile keepers from Australia Zoo had been

invited along to see how it was done and to lend an experienced hand. Robert's mum was an expert with crocodiles, just like his dad had been, and Robert and Riley were experienced Wildlife Warriors with a taste for adventure.

The Cisco Swamp was the biggest in Texas and the survey would continue for a whole week. There were now so many alligators it was hard to believe that only forty years ago they had been hunted almost to the brink of extinction. In 1967 they'd been listed as an endangered species, but thanks to monitoring and

protection from various fish and wildlife agencies, the population of American alligators had recovered so well that by 1987 they were removed from the list. To a Wildlife Warrior, it didn't get much better than that.

As part of the research, each alligator had to be tagged, measured and have its weight estimated. Nests were uncovered and eggs were counted so that they could predict how big the population might be the following year. With some of the bigger alligators measuring up to 4.5 metres and weighing over

300 kilograms, restraining them was exhausting and dangerous work.

The boys had been making themselves useful all morning, logging all the research information into a graph. It was going to take pride of place in the alligator project that they were working on for school. But now as it inched towards lunchtime they were tired, and mischief was getting harder to avoid. Within minutes the alligator poo was flying again and this time Robert wasn't quick enough to avoid it!

# CHAPTER TWO

'Riley! That smells so bad!' yelled Robert, wiping his hands on his shirt and pretending to storm off in disgust. But as Riley caught up to him Robert took a perfect dive to the ground and rolled backwards, knocking Riley completely off his feet.

'Eat dirt, Riley! Perfect payback. I think that deserves a round of applause,' declared Robert as he took a bow.

But Riley was not the sort to take these things lying down. Once Robert's back was turned he was on his feet like lightning. With his head down he threw his whole body weight against his friend and hung on around his waist until they had both barrelled to the ground.

'I think that's ten out of ten for the perfect deathroll!' Riley yelled gleefully as they rolled once and then again before coming to a clattering stop against the

camp table that they'd set up for their project. The table went down and all their hard work with it. Pens, pencils, rulers and rubbers flew everywhere and the whole folder of work, including the graph, lay in the mud.

'Oh no,' said Riley and Robert at the same time. They were almost as muddy as their work but set about trying to right the table and reverse the damage as quickly as they could.

Although they weren't quick enough.

'Okay, that's it, you two!' yelled Scott, as he stormed over for the second time.

The boys got to their feet, trying to look dignified, though they realised that this time they'd gone too far. Riley was no longer smiling.

'Mum's here too,' murmured Robert, already regretting how silly he had been. Terri was right behind Scott.

'Robert, I'm surprised at you!' said Terri. She sounded disappointed rather than angry. 'You and Riley are really stepping out of line. We're here to do a job, mate, and we can't do that if we have to worry about you both, can we?'

'No, Mum,' said Robert. It wasn't

often that Terri had to tell them off and he felt really awful about the whole thing.

'Now, we have another hour or so until lunch,' said Terri briskly. 'I suggest you two go back to the tent and clean yourselves up. Then you can report to Dan in the kitchen tent and volunteer your services for the rest of the afternoon. I don't want to see either one of you within 50 metres of this swamp. All right?'

The boys mumbled their agreement as they gathered up all the soggy pages of the project and shuffled away in disgrace. Scott and Terri gave the boys an approving nod before walking off.

'This is completely your fault, Riley!' whispered Robert angrily.

'How do you figure? You pushed me first, remember?' said Riley.

But the best friends never bickered for long and once they were clean(ish) again, they introduced themselves to Dan in the mess tent.

Dan sat them down with an icy cold lemonade each and a whole pile of cutlery to roll up in serviettes. There were worse things they could be doing.

'Hey, my grandad's been here, you know,' said Robert, back to his normal chatty self.

'Texas?' asked Riley.

'No, actually here at Cisco Swamp,' said Robert. 'We have a great picture at home of him with his biggest catch ever when he was really young. It was an alligator gar that was almost 2 metres long! That's one of the reasons I wanted to come. I'd love to see one.'

'Well, surely you've seen enough of them today to last you a lifetime!' said Riley.

'Not an alligator, Riley. An alligator *gar*. It's a fish, not a reptile. It's called that because its teeth and mouth look a lot like an alligator's. But it has the body of a fish,' explained Robert.

'So did your grandad eat the big alligator gar he caught?' asked Riley.

'I don't know,' said Robert. 'I doubt it, though. They have really hard scales. It's as if they're armoured for protection. The Native Americans back then used the scales as the pointy bits of their arrows. They're prehistoric too! Scientists reckon they've been around since the Cretaceous period. It's about the closest you could get to an actual living dinosaur. I wonder if they've changed much in that time?' he pondered.

'Ha! I knew you'd get round to dinosaurs before long. You're obsessed!' said Riley, rolling his eyes to heaven. He could tell from experience that Robert was just getting into his stride.

'Hey boys! I need a volunteer if you've finished over there!' shouted Dan from the other side of the tent. 'These bread rolls aren't going to butter themselves.'

17

'I'll do it, Dan,' said Riley, jumping up. 'Catch you later, Robert!'

Robert knew that Riley wasn't all that interested in dinosaurs, but he just couldn't help talking about them anyway. I'll have to do a page or two about alligator gar in the project, he thought to himself. They really were fascinating fish.

He could hear Riley starting to chat with Dan about dirt bikes and thought, Riley was pretty obsessed himself! Then the sound of the voices seemed to wobble and fade and Robert started to feel dizzy and a bit disorientated.

'Must be the heat,' thought Robert, and he staggered silently out of the tent to get some fresh air.

# CHAPTER THREE

But it wasn't the heat.

Robert was sure he had felt something like this before, but could it really be happening again? He put his hand to the prehistoric claw, which he always carried in his pocket. It had been there for ages now, since he'd found it months ago in Winton.

What a weird day that had been! He'd felt dizzy just like this and then he'd found himself running through a Cretaceous forest after a stampede of ornithopods and coelurosaurs, only to have come face-to-face with a fearsome *australovenator*.

For days afterwards he had been both excited and a bit worried that he might find himself back in prehistoric times at any moment. In fact, he'd taken to carrying a snack with him always, just in case. But no matter how hard he wished and hoped, he couldn't make it happen again. Yet deep down he'd been

sure that the claw had something to do with it.

And now here he was, on the other side of the world, and the claw in his hand was feeling tingly. Robert suddenly felt faint and could feel himself falling.

Wow, it really was happening again!

*Where will I end up this time?* he wondered before landing with a soft bump. As his head cleared he looked at the claw. It looked exactly as it had the day he'd unearthed it. But as Robert put it away into his pocket, he knew it was no normal dinosaur fossil.

Time travelling back to prehistoric Winton had seemed almost like a dream, yet he'd recorded some of the things he'd seen on his digital voice recorder and had played them over and over again since then, just to remind himself that the whole thing had really happened. As he thought back, he patted his pocket. His trusty recorder was there. Phew!

But Robert didn't even have time to think about getting it out. Before he'd taken so much as a single step into what looked like Cretaceous swampland, he

heard an awful roar coming from directly behind him.

His natural instinct told him to run away as fast as he could, but instead he breathed in deeply. He knew enough about animals to realise that running away was a sure sign to anything watching that you were prey.

Robert summoned up all of his courage and turned around slowly.

# CHAPTER FOUR

When Robert saw what he was now almost face-to-face with, his mouth became dry and he could feel his heart beating in his chest. He'd read just about every book ever written on dinosaurs and he had no doubt at all that the huge reptile about 40 metres from where he

stood was the mighty *Deinosuchus* (dai-no-sook-uss) – one of the largest of the prehistoric crocodiles!

His mind reeled as he tried to remember everything he'd read about it. He could see the picture in his book back home. *The Big Book of Dinosaurs* had got it pretty spot-on, considering only a handful of *deinosuchus* bones had ever been found. One of those was a jaw bone, which was 2 metres in length! Robert could now see why the *deinosuchus* had had such a huge jaw – so that it could match the rest of his huge body!

The roaring continued and Robert felt a moment of relief when he realised that it wasn't directed at him. In fact, the *deinosuchus* didn't seem to have noticed him at all. It was roaring almost continuously and thrashing about on the banks of the huge swamp. The sand and mud surrounding him were churned up, and it looked as if the huge beast had been struggling for a long time.

Robert was torn between sheer admiration for the enormous animal and utter terror. He was used to seeing crocodiles, of course, but this one must

have been 15 metres long! It looked similar to the alligators he'd been seeing all week but on a much bigger scale. The *deinosuchus* was at least three or four times the size of the biggest alligator or crocodile he had ever seen. What *was* it doing?

But that didn't matter. It was more important to be thankful for what it *wasn't* doing. And at this moment in time it was quite wonderful that it *wasn't* eating Robert.

Realising that his luck could change at any moment, Robert started inching

backwards carefully, hoping to find a safe place where he could watch what was happening without being seen. With his eyes firmly on the prehistoric predator, his progress was painfully slow, but bit by bit the gap between them got bigger.

Robert's breathing was just getting back to normal when he stumbled backwards over the roots of a mangrove tree and he fell to the ground with an involuntary cry. In front of him, the *deinosuchus* stopped its struggling and snapped to attention.

For a split second everything was still and silent as Robert stared into the yellow reptilian eyes of the *deinosuchus*.

# CHAPTER FIVE

'Keep calm, keep calm, keep calm,' Robert thought as he stood up quickly and bounded towards the mangrove tree, shinning up it like a demented koala. The *deinosuchus* had covered the ground between them with effortless speed and was already hot on Robert's trail.

Luckily the tree was a good one for climbing and Robert had had plenty of practice. He didn't so much as pause for breath until he was a good 10 or 12 metres above the ground on a branch that was as wide as himself.

What now? he thought, once he'd got his breath back.

The *deinosuchus* was circling the base of the tree but not with any sense of urgency. Robert started to feel a little optimistic that it was either not very hungry or it simply hadn't recognised him as something tasty to eat.

Robert wasn't certain what to do next but felt sure he'd think of something soon. In the meantime, the *deinosuchus* had started up with the roaring again. It was thrashing about as though its life depended on it.

Robert took out his digital voice recorder and delivered an update. 'Well, it's happening again! I think I'm still beside Cisco Swamp but I don't know what year it is. There's a *deinosuchus* under the tree that I'm in and I'm hoping he's not too hungry. I guess that makes it sometime during the late Cretaceous

period. This is one huge croc! He's behaving really weirdly too, though that could be normal for a *deinosuchus*. Oh, wait a sec –' He put the recorder back in his pocket and looked carefully at the reptile below.

He *had* seen that sort of behaviour before. Of course he had! On Australia Zoo's most recent croc research trip, he'd seen a saltwater crocodile with a jaw injury act just like that! It was the behaviour of an animal in serious pain.

Once he realised the truth of the matter, Robert could see the *deinosuchus* as just another animal – one that he might be able to help.

The *deinosuchus* was still pacing and thrashing about at the base of the tree, and from the safety of his perch Robert was able to really examine him from nose to tail. He searched for any obviously broken bones or cuts or gashes in its thick skin. But there was nothing. It was only when the *deinosuchus* looked up and actually made eye contact with him again that he realised its mouth was still wide open. It seemed as though he couldn't shut it!

Robert spotted the good-sized stick that was jammed into the *deinosuchus's* mouth like a prop. Its mouth was bleeding badly, and it was beginning to look as though the poor creature's struggles were coming close to their natural end.

Robert could see that the dinosaur was beginning to tire. His fear had gone now and had been replaced with pure sympathy. It must be so frustrating for the *deinosuchus*! Not to mention dangerous. Robert was well aware that even something as big as a *deinosuchus* would become tired very quickly if it

couldn't fight back. And looking out over the swamp, he could see many huge pairs of nostrils dotted around. It was as though all the other *deinosuchuses* for miles around were queuing up for an easy meal.

Okay, thought Robert. Time to put the brain to work. How could he possibly remove that stick from the *deinosuchus's* mouth without getting himself munched in the process? There was no way he was going down there! It may have been a long time since the *deinosuchus* last had a good meal, and

there was no way he was providing it with home delivery service!

Robert would have to do something from up here . . . but what?

# CHAPTER SIX

After a few minutes of deep thought, the tree vines that hung down around Robert provided him with a bit of inspiration. After gathering armfuls of the long, thin vines he set about plaiting them together.

More than once he wished he'd paid more attention to his sister Bindi and her braided hairstyles, as he painstakingly crossed one vine over the other, again and again and again. After what seemed like ages, he had fashioned a reasonable-looking length of thin rope. He knotted a sturdy stick to one end and secured the other end to the solid branch that he was sitting on.

Robert was as pleased as punch with his plan so far! Now all he had to do was persuade the *deinosuchus* to stand still and open its mouth wide, while he launched the stick-on-a-string deep into his mouth, lodged it behind the stuck

stick and then pulled it out! What could be easier?

Well, it was worth a go anyway. First he had to try to get the *deinosuchus* to stop pacing and start concentrating on the boy-sized meal in the tree. They needed to be pretty much face-to-face if this was going to work.

Robert shouted into the silent swamp, 'Hey, hey, big guy! I'm up here!'

Then he started a slow rhythmic drumming with his feet and his stick, yelling the whole time. The *deinosuchus* found a burst of energy from somewhere

and rounded on Robert. He was furious.

'That's right!' yelled Robert. 'You should be angry. Now keep looking this way. Nice and wide . . .'

Robert unravelled his rope but as it dangled down in front of the enormous mouth, the *deinosuchus* sent it swinging and Robert had to steady himself and start over.

The giant croc seemed determined to get at him, as it slammed its head against the trunk, causing the whole tree to shake.

'Okay, this is the one,' murmured

Robert to himself as the huge jaws gaped ten metres below.

His hand was steady. This time, instead of unwinding the rope, he just threw the stick straight down and hoped the rope wouldn't get knotted. It didn't. It was perfect!

The stick-on-a-string lodged in firmly behind the stuck stick in the huge mouth and the *deinosuchus* let out a huge roar as it backed up. And backed up. And backed up. Robert looked in alarm as his pile of rope got smaller and smaller. The stick wasn't popping out!

Within seconds the rope was completely taut and still the stick hadn't moved. The *deinosuchus* was still thrashing and pulling about when Robert heard the first creak.

His branch was bending!

The stick was clearly very stuck indeed but Robert only had time for a flicker of sympathy for the pained animal before he started to panic for himself. The thick branch was looking less safe by the second.

'Surely the rope will snap first? Why did I tie it to the branch? Why did I make

it so strong?' he thought, before the loudest creak yet.

Robert realised that the time for keeping his fingers crossed was over. He needed to find a way out and he needed to do it now! But just as he was starting to scurry sideways towards the trunk there was a loud snap. The branch sprung upwards and Robert went with it.

# CHAPTER SEVEN

Robert landed, stunned, but in one piece amid the mangrove roots. The rope-vine was bunched all around him, and looking round he could see the stick on the end, coated with blood.

'It worked!'

He celebrated for a second before

spotting the *deinosuchus*, which seemed similarly stunned. The giant croc flexed his bloody jaw and let out an enormous roar.

It felt a little too close for comfort and Robert quickly considered his options. But there were only two he could think of: Fight or flight?

He had a brief fantasy of going for the 'fight' option until he pictured the two of them in battle. Though he wasn't small for his age, his 30 kilogram body weight quite possibly made him a 'flea-weight' compared to the tonnes of sinewy croc

in front of him. Crikey, it could probably swallow him whole!

Flight it was, then. Happy with his decision, Robert sprinted along the sandy strand before ducking into a little thicket of closely packed tree ferns. They towered above him and, as he paused for a breather before deciding on his next step, he could see the wide expanse of sky. A flock of pterosaurs was spinning and wheeling miles above his head. Wow, this place was just unreal!

He peered out of the thicket in the direction he had come from. He was

almost confident that the *deinosuchus* hadn't followed him, but he wanted to be sure. Thankfully, it was nowhere to be seen. Just as he was about to breathe a sigh of relief, he began to sense something else.

What was it?

He stood up and listened as hard as he could. It wasn't a noise so much as a sensation; he could feel it in his feet.

There was a faint tremor in the ground. It was a full couple of minutes before his ears could register the noise, by which time it had become a rhythmic pulse that could only be described as footsteps. But they were huge ones and they were coming fast.

Robert was certain that it wasn't the *deinosuchus* – the footfalls sounded as though they came from a two-legged creature – and as the noise grew closer and more deafening, it became clear that whatever was approaching was far bigger.

# CHAPTER EIGHT

Robert had another quick decision to make. Running towards the noise would be madness. Staying put seemed almost as bad, and returning to the swamp seemed very dangerous indeed. Even if the *deinosuchus* had gone for a swim away from shore, there were dozens more out in the swamp, waiting to take its place.

Robert reached for the claw in his pocket. It seemed weird now to think he'd thought it was responsible for sending him here. It was an impressive-looking claw but that was all. It lay there, dusty and dry in his hand. It certainly didn't appear as though it was something that could get him home again anytime soon. Clutching the claw to his chest, he wished silently to go home now, please!

For a split second he really thought

it was going to work, but there was no dizzy feeling.

Time was really running out. The trees around him had started to shake with every footfall and Robert realised he was right in the path of whatever was coming. He took a deep breath and ran back down the strand towards the swamp. All he could think of was the *deinosuchus*'s eyes as boy and dinosaur had stared at each other earlier on.

The swamp was still and empty, but Robert couldn't forget the sheer number of nostrils he'd seen looming here earlier.

Were all the accompanying eyes staring at him right at this moment?

The mangrove tree was ahead and he managed to get behind the trunk just as the huge dinosaur broke through the tree line. Robert could hardly believe his eyes. It was *Albertosaurus* (al-burt-o-sore-us), in all its terrifying glory.

Its huge solid legs were almost three times Robert's height and width. No wonder it had made such a racket! The whole body was a whopping 8 metres long from its head to the tip of its muscular tail. Its broad head

was huge and box-like and seemed full of teeth that surely meant business.

The front arms were less impressive – they hung limp and useless from high up on the carnivore's body, with two measly claws on each arm. Robert knew the *albertosaurus* wasn't going to need them to fight.

Robert stood perfectly still. He wondered about the dinosaur's sight and sense of smell. Could it sniff him out from where he was standing? Was that how they hunted their food? One of the biggest, deadliest carnivores of all time and it was standing just there!

As he watched, the *albertosaurus* seemed to pause and sniff the air. Then, cautiously, it approached the edge of the swamp and ventured in, up to its huge ankles. Then it stopped. What was it doing? It didn't appear to be drinking, just waiting.

There was a furious splashing at the water's edge. The *albertosaurus* was as still as a statue but in its mouth was another big creature, which flailed and flapped for a minute or two till it stopped.

The *albertosaurus* was fishing! The 'fish' was enormous! Even in the jaws of this giant predator it looked big and was easily 4 or 5 metres long with a solid body. As far as Robert knew, it was *spinosaurus* that was known to eat fish, not *albertosaurus*. How fascinating! As the *albertosaurus* tossed its prey back and forth, chomping huge chunks, Robert caught sight of its head.

'Alligator gar,' thought Robert. That's what the *albertosaurus* was fishing for! So they *were* prehistoric, and not much seemed to have changed for the fish, appearance-wise, since the Cretaceous period!

The prehistoric alligator gar's mouth resembled that of a modern alligator but with an unmistakably fish-like long snout. It was much bigger than the modern-day alligator gar, and judging by the speed with which the *albertosaurus* was eating it, it wasn't very well armoured either. Maybe the sharp arrowhead scales had only evolved later?

Robert felt a twinge of sympathy for the alligator gar but couldn't help marvelling at the thought that this fish

had been food 75 million years ago and had also survived the same event that had caused the extinction of *albertosaurus* millions of years after. He'd be pretty close to the top of the food chain now, thought Robert.

He recorded a quick update on the voice recorder when the *albertosaurus*'s huge head snapped up. It had heard something. Abandoning the half-eaten gar, the *albertosaurus* backed out of the water and turned to face Robert's direction.

Robert stared at the huge head with blood-stained teeth, and froze to the spot as the enormous carnivore started to run clumsily towards him.

Out of the corner of his eye, Robert saw a flash of movement and heard a terrible sound. The *deinosuchus* was almost fully out of the water before Robert had even noticed that it was there. The *albertosaurus* spotted it at exactly the same moment. It's not every day you see a dinosaur do a double-take, but that's how it happened and Robert took note of the fact.

The *albertosaurus* tried to run, but it was too late. Its only option was to fight back. Its huge jaws slammed shut on thin air while the *deinosuchus* grabbed it by the throat and effortlessly pulled the huge predator back into the deeper water, where it performed the deathroll that Robert was so familiar with from the crocs back home.

The swamp was eerily still for a few moments and then erupted once more in a frenzy of thrashing and churning as all the outlying *deinosuchuses* spotted an easy meal after all. They swarmed towards the struggling *albertosaurus*.

Maybe this terrifying demonstration was enough to make it clear that *albertosauruses* should not go fishing – being at the water's edge was just too dangerous for one of the biggest carnivores of all time!

# CHAPTER NINE

The swarming *deinosuchuses* created a huge surge of water that washed Robert off the bank and straight into the murky, muddy water.

'Aarrgh,' screamed Robert, shutting his eyes and clutching onto the dinosaur fossil, hoping for a miracle of some sort.

'Robert Clarence Irwin!' shouted his mother, seconds later.

Robert opened his eyes and found himself flat on his back, 20 metres from the lunch tent. He was wet and muddy from top to toe and he had never before been so happy to be told off.

'Water!' he shouted gleefully. 'It's definitely water!'

'Yes, Robert, and we use it for washing,' said Terri patiently. 'Perhaps you could go and experience it for yourself, right now!'

By now, the whole lunch queue was looking their way and grinning.

Robert would have been cringing with embarrassment if he hadn't been so utterly relieved to be alive.

'Sorry, Mum, I'll go and get changed,' he said, and surprised Terri by attempting to give her a hug.

'Maybe try out the water thing first?' she suggested, stepping back quickly to keep him and his slime at arm's length.

Robert looked down at himself and grinned. 'You have a point,' he said, and headed off to his tent.

Riley fell into step with him before he'd gone more than a few metres away

from the queue. 'So?' he said, looking suspiciously at Robert.

'What?' said Robert.

Riley wiggled his eyebrows but Robert played dumb.

'So, explain yourself, mate. You disappear for 15 minutes and leave me, your best friend, to do the work of two men! That Dan is a real slavedriver you know!' said Riley indignantly.

'Fifteen minutes?' said Robert, incredulous. 'Was that how long I've been gone for?'

'Fifteen minutes is a long time

in kitchen-time, I'm telling you! So what happened? How did you end up covered in mud? Have you been off having adventures without me?' accused Riley.

Robert stopped walking and pondered for a long moment. He was just busting to tell someone, and who better than Riley? They'd been best friends since forever and he knew he could be absolutely trusted to keep quiet on this. Mind you, he'd never had a secret like this to keep before.

'Robert!' said Riley. 'Hello! Are you

in there?' he said, clicking his fingers in front of his friend's face.

Robert looked solemnly at Riley and made his decision. 'Riley, what I'm about to tell you is going to sound really weird, but you have to promise to listen all the way to the end. Okay? And you can't tell anyone! Not even your dad.'

Riley looked surprised but nodded without hesitation.

'It all started the day that I found this in Winton . . .' Robert began. He took the prehistoric claw from his pocket and handed it to Riley.

# CHAPTER TEN

Robert kept back nothing.

By the end of the story Riley was completely agog. He stared at Robert and at the claw and seemed completely blown away. Both boys were silent for the longest time.

'So . . . ?' said Robert eventually.

'Wow,' said Riley.

'It is wow,' agreed Robert. 'Seriously wow. There's no better word!'

'You should write this stuff down, you know. I'm sure there's a multimillion dollar book deal out there just waiting for you. Where do you get it? You're so obsessed with dinosaurs that you're starting to dream about them!' Riley laughed and threw the claw back to Robert.

'But, Riley, it happened! Twice now, too!' cried Robert.

'So prove it!' said Riley, thinking that that would end the conversation.

'Okay, I will,' said Robert, standing up.

'And how will you do that exactly?' asked Riley.

'Well, the next time it happens you'll just have to come with me,' said Robert, both pleased with himself for thinking of it and a bit worried that it might not be possible. But why not? If he could travel back in time, why couldn't Riley come too?

'You're nuts,' said Riley, as he walked off on his own to get his lunch.

81

When Robert came into the lunch tent ten minutes later, Riley was still thinking. He was a bit worried about Robert. It wasn't like him to take things so seriously. Maybe he had a touch of heatstroke?

But, thought Riley, they were best friends. And best friends stuck together. What was the worst that could happen? Well, he could end up completely obsessed with dinosaurs. The only really unlikely thing would be that he'd be stuck in a parallel universe with only a *triceratops* for company.

He decided to give Robert the benefit of the doubt.

'Hey Robert, have you tried the fruit salad? I made it myself,' he called over to his friend.

Robert grabbed some lunch and went to sit with Riley. He looked nervous.

'So . . .?' said Riley, smiling.

'Huh?' said Robert.

'So, you've no idea when it's going to happen or where you're going to end up?' asked Riley.

'Nope, no idea at all,' said Robert cautiously. 'I hold the claw and then just

feel woozy, like I'm falling,' said Robert.

'Okay. Go on,' said Riley.

'So far I don't think I travel anywhere new. I think I stay right where I am and it's time that moves. Today I'm pretty sure I was still here in Cisco Swamp,' said Robert excitedly.

'Too weird,' said Riley, shaking his head again as though he was trying to clear it. 'Well, it's decided then!' he said decisively.

'What?' said Robert.

'I'm going to have to be on woozy-alert all summer. If you're going to

disappear back a few million years, then you'd better have some reliable company. Don't you think?' asked Riley.

'Agreed!' said Robert, relieved.

At that moment Scott passed the boys on his way to lunch. 'Hey you two, fancy some fishing later? There are alligator gar the size of our crocs out there,' he said.

Robert gave an involuntary shudder, thinking back to the fate of the albertosaurus that thought a bit of fish for lunch would be nice. 'Thanks, Scott,' he said, 'but I think I'm safer sticking with the fruit salad for now.'

FIELD GUIDE

Drawn by Robert Irwin

# ALBERTOSAURUS

GENUS: *Tyrannosauroid Therepod*

ETYMOLOGY: Alberta-Lizard. Alberta was the Canadian province where this dinosaur was first discovered. They named it in the province's honour! And Saurus is Greek for 'lizard'.

DISCOVERED: First bones discovered in 1884. Henry Fairfield Osborn discovered more in Alberta, Canada in 1905 and that's when it got its name.

HOME: North America

PERIOD: Late Cretaceous period,
approximately 75 million years ago

LENGTH: 8 metres long

HEIGHT: 3.5 metres high

WEIGHT: Approximately 2 tonnes

MOST FAMOUS RELATIVE: Tyrannosaurus Rex

DIET: Strictly carnivore and top of the food
chain

Albertosaurus was a huge animal, but was only about half the size of his more famous cousin the T-Rex.

They looked similar with a broad head and a short muscular body. Their thick tails helped with balance and agility, enabling them to run fast and turn quickly. Their legs were like thick pillars but were bird-like at the hips with three toes on each foot. They ran like birds too, on two legs.

Albertosaurus also had two tiny arms with two fingers on each hand, though it's a bit of a mystery what they used them for  their arms were so short they couldn't even reach their mouths!

# DEINOSUCHUS

ETYMOLOGY: *Deinos* comes from the Greek word for 'terrible' and *soukhos* from the Greek word for 'crocodile'. So, put together, deinosuchus means 'terrible crocodile'.

DISCOVERED: Teeth were first discovered in North Carolina in 1858. But because they so resembled regular crocodile teeth, no one took a close look at them until 1903, when some big scales turned up too.

*Deinosuchus* didn't even have an official name until 1909, when W.J. Holland thought someone had better name it something!

HOME: *Deinosuchus* remains have been found in ten of the United States, including Montana, Alabama and Texas, as well as Mexico.

PERIOD: Late Cretaceous period, 80–73 million years ago

LENGTH: Up to 15 metres long

WEIGHT: Up to 8 tonnes

DIET: Carnivorous and not too fussy. Would have eaten lots of fish and turtles, as well as any unfortunate dinosaurs that got too close to the water.

*Deinosuchus* would have ruled the waters of the USA. They have been found on both sides of the Western Interior Seaway, which was a huge body of water that stretched from the top to the bottom of North America, effectively dividing the continent in two. At places it was almost 1000 kilometres wide.

*Deinosuchus* looked and behaved very much the same as modern-day crocodiles and alligators. Recent discoveries suggest that, like all crocodilians, *deinosuchus* continued to grow throughout the course of its life. It just carried on right past adulthood and kept getting more and more massive! Some of them may have lived for about 100 years.

# ARMOURED DEFENCE

## WRITTEN BY JACK WELLS

RANDOM HOUSE AUSTRALIA

# CHAPTER ONE

'Awesome! We're 26 metres off the ground up here!' Robert shouted out excitedly, taking in the view. 'Look, Riley, those people down there are smaller than ants. They're like microscopic amoeba or something. Amazing!'

Robert's best friend, on the other

hand, was looking a little green around the gills and refused to look down. He kept his eyes very firmly on the horizon. 'Please don't mention how high up we are,' Riley mumbled.

'Twenty-six metres equals about 86 feet. Does that sound better to you?'

Riley considered this for a moment. 'If I think of it as 86 of *my* feet, that doesn't sound so bad.'

Robert chuckled. 'Whatever works for you, buddy.'

Recently, Robert's life had changed quite dramatically after he'd found

a magic fossil that allowed him to travel back to the Age of Dinosaurs. But never in his wildest dreams had he ever considered being able to stand in the mouth of the world's largest T-rex!

Of course, this wasn't a *real* T-rex. It was a huge steel replica of one but, just like the big pineapple in Queensland, this T-rex was bigger than the real thing – four and a half times bigger to be exact. From the statue's open jaw, tourists could survey the famous Canadian Badlands, home of the largest amount of

dinosaur fossil discoveries in the world.

'When I told Uncle Nate you were a dinosaur hunter, he knew you'd love it here in Alberta,' said Riley.

Robert and Riley's families had travelled from Texas, USA to spend a few days at Calgary Zoo, helping to look after some newborn red pandas. Riley's Uncle Nate, who'd lived in Canada since he'd graduated high school, had offered to take the boys on a two-day camping trip in the Canadian Badlands.

'You're gonna love Uncle Nate. He's someone really high up in the Canadian

Army – a general, or maybe even a president or something.'

'I'm not sure you can be a president in the army, can you?' asked Robert.

Riley shrugged. 'Maybe they created a special position for Uncle Nate because he's so good.'

'Maybe,' replied Robert a little doubtfully.

'He's so strong and tough, and he's fought in lots of wars and you don't want to mess with him,' said Riley proudly.

'Mess with who?' said a gruff voice from behind them.

'Uncle Nate!' cried Riley, as his uncle lifted him up and spun him around.

'How's my favourite nephew?' Uncle Nate asked, lowering Riley to the ground and holding on to him till he regained his balance. 'I saw your dad down in the car park and he said I'd find you here.'

'I've grown since you saw me last, haven't I?' said Riley, trying to hide his dizziness. It was hard enough being up this high, but getting spun around too?! He wasn't going to look like a wuss in front of his uncle.

'One day you might grow to be as big as your favourite relative,' Uncle Nate said with a laugh. He turned to Robert. 'And you must be the famous Robert Irwin who Riley always talks about.'

Riley frowned. 'I don't always talk about him,' he admonished. 'Sometimes I talk about dirt-biking, and snakes and rugby league and termite mounds . . .'

Uncle Nate interrupted, knowing that when Riley started talking, it was sometimes hard to get him to stop. 'Yes, perhaps Robert's not your only topic of

conversation.' He shook Robert's hand. 'Nice to meet you, son.'

'G'day, I've heard a lot about you too, Uncle Nate.'

After days and days of Riley talking about his uncle as this awesomely strong and tough army bloke, it was surprising to Robert that the man in front of him was not the size of a *titanosaur*, or even an *albertosaurus*. Uncle Nate was shorter than average and fit-looking, but not covered in muscles like Robert had imagined. He had a big friendly smile and cropped sandy brown hair.

Uncle Nate chuckled. 'Oh, yeah? It better be good stuff or Riley will be digging the latrines at the camp site.'

Riley looked horrified. 'It was all good stuff, wasn't it, Robert? Tell him. Only good stuff.'

Uncle Nate and Robert laughed as the three of them made their way from the viewing platform and began the hike back down to ground level.

# CHAPTER TWO

'Tell Robert about the last time you were in Afghanistan, Uncle Nate,' said Riley as the boys put their seatbelts on.

Uncle Nate manoeuvred the station wagon out of the car park and they hit the open road. 'What do you want to know?'

'Did you fight the enemy and lock them all up?' prompted Riley.

Uncle Nate gave a tired grin. 'It's a bit more complicated than that, buddy. We're over there to help train the national security forces. We're not involved in combat in Afghanistan any more.'

'So you teach the good guys to shoot guns and protect the local people from the bad guys?' Riley's eyes were bugging out of his head.

'Yeah, sure. Something like that. The last trip to Kabul, there was a situation that could've turned deadly . . .'

While Riley hung on his uncle's every word, Robert's mind drifted back to dinosaurs. He took his special fossil out from his pocket, holding it carefully in the palm of his hand. He carried it with him all the time, along with a digital voice recorder, which he used to document the weird and wonderful things he saw on his travels.

The fossil didn't look magical. And most of the time it wasn't. He was never sure when it would transport him back in time, but he figured that since he was

in prime dinosaur territory, it could happen at any moment.

In Texas, after seeing a *deinosuchus* take on an *albertosaurus*, he couldn't keep the time travel a secret any longer. He'd told Riley about the fossil and promised him that, if he could, he'd take his friend along with him the next time. Robert had had no idea if he'd be able to do it, but Riley would never forgive him if he didn't try. He just hoped the fossil didn't send him time-travelling while he was in a moving car!

'. . . it was dangerous and a couple of my soldiers needed bandages and lice treatment, but we got out all right.'

Riley was grinning at his uncle as though he was the best thing since the invention of the dirt bike. 'That's an awesome story, Uncle Nate.'

'Before we get to the camp site, take a look out the window. The badlands are like nowhere else on earth,' said Uncle Nate.

Robert pocketed his fossil and returned to the conversation. 'I've been wondering why this place is called the badlands in the first place.'

Riley sniggered. 'It sounds like the kind of place where cowboys have shootouts.'

'Badlands are areas that are pretty much dry. The rock is soft and has been eroded by the rain and wind, causing some cool geologicial formations to pop up over time,' Uncle Nate explained.

'Like that one?' Robert pointed to a tall rock sculpture, which looked as though it had a mushroom-cup head.

'Exactly. They're called *hoodoos*. The rock on the top is iron stone. It's harder than the rock beneath it, so the pillar has been worn away. The erosion creates a whole lot of interesting shapes.'

'So the extreme erosion in this area has helped uncover dinosaur fossils?' asked Robert, peering out the car window, quietly hoping to catch sight of an *albertosaurus* skeleton lying by the side of the road. Instead there was only a patch of dry grass.

'That's right. They've found a whole range of dinosaur fossils here. From *triceratops* to *stegosaurs* –'

'*Albertosaurus* and T-rex,' piped up Riley.

'And one of my favourite anklyosaurs, *Euoplocephalus* (you-oh-ploe-seff-ah-luss), has been found here too,' added Robert.

'Is he the guy who looked like an armoured tank?' asked Uncle Nate, overtaking a caravan with a trailer attached. It was peak tourist season and Dinosaur Provincial Park was teeming with holiday-makers.

'That's him, all right. The *euoplocephalus* was covered in protective plates and had a club-like tail. He didn't seem that impressive, but he definitely knew how to stand up for himself.'

Uncle Nate nodded. 'Sounds a bit like me, actually. There are a lot of guys in the army that are bigger and stronger, but sometimes it's the little guys that come up with good defensive tactics.'

Riley scoffed. 'There's nothing interesting about defence. It's all about the attack.' With that, Riley launched himself at Robert, pretending to bite his friend on the neck.

'Ahhhh, get off me.' Robert giggled and tried to defend himself. It was a hard thing to do wearing a seatbelt and not being able to move more than a couple of centimetres away from Riley.

Uncle Nate looked in the rear-view mirror, smiling at the two boys. In his most authoritative voice, he barked, 'Soldiers. The camp site is 15 minutes away. No further attacks on each other until we're out of the car.'

'Yes, sir!' the two boys replied in unison, sitting up straight with eyes ahead.

# CHAPTER THREE

The camp site was at the edge of a small lake. More strangely shaped hoodoos in the distance cast interesting shadows over the surrounding grasslands. Riley and Robert were sitting on a couple of foldaway chairs, eating vegemite sandwiches. Uncle Nate had gone off in

search of some cold drinks, leaving the boys to soak up the beautiful and unusual environment.

Riley gobbled up his sandwich first and went to grab the rest of his friend's food. But Robert was too quick. He shoved the rest of the sandwich into his mouth before Riley could get to it. 'Too late, mate,' he said with his mouth full.

'It's never too late for an attack!' With a grin, Riley launched himself again at his friend.

At that moment, Robert felt the

familiar tingle of his fossil. He reached into his pocket, holding the fossil in both hands, a second before Riley landed on him. Before Robert could warn him, the two friends disappeared into the now familiar vortex, falling through time, with Riley still yelling his vegemite war cry. 'Waaaaaa . . .'

'. . . aaaaaahat just happened?!' finished Riley a few moments later, lying breathless on the ground. He looked around him, confused. There were no

longer any foldaway chairs or a tent nearby, or any sign of hoodoos in the distance. Thankfully, though, his best friend was sprawled on the ground next to him.

Riley grabbed his head. 'Man, I feel like someone just chucked me into an angry washing machine.'

Robert stood up warily, glancing at his fossil before pocketing it. 'Riley, mate, you've just time-travelled.'

'Eh?'

'Gone back in time about 70 million years,' Robert explained further.

Riley's eyes widened. 'No way.' But as he glanced around, he realised Robert knew exactly what he was talking about. 'This is epic!'

Robert was all business. He took out his voice recorder and pressed record. 'I've time-travelled, and this time Riley's here with me.'

Riley turned and waved as though the voice recorder was a video recorder.

Robert rolled his eyes good-naturedly. 'I suspect we may have travelled back to the Cretaceous period again, probably still in Alberta.'

Riley whipped around. 'You mean there are *albertosauruses* here?' All of a sudden he wasn't feeling so thrilled to have time-travelled.

Robert nodded. 'Remember that they've found over 35 types of dinosaur fossils in this area, and that might just be a small portion of the animals that roamed these parts.'

'Okay, but tell me there were more herbivores than carnivores here. Please?'

Robert shrugged. 'Half and half. What's interesting is that the herbivores from this era were heavily armoured.'

'To protect themselves from lots of ferocious meat-eaters?' suggested Riley nervously.

Robert nodded.

'Well then, I think it might be time to go back. We don't want to keep Uncle Nate waiting,' said Riley, hopping from one foot to the next.

Robert slung his arm around his friend's shoulder. 'Let's just have a quick look around first. See what's happening.'

Riley tried to be reassured by his friend's relaxed nature. 'Okay. But this

doesn't look like the badlands that we were driving through, does it?'

Robert surveyed the landscape. Riley was right. There were none of the rocky formations that were everywhere in the badlands of modern times. The boys could make out an internal sea, which Robert had read was called the Bearpaw Sea, off in the distance. And closer to them, the ground was swampy, with long matted reeds dotted around the edge of the swamps.

The boys had to tread carefully, and Robert led the way, looking out for

creatures with large teeth and murderous intent. He was heading towards a forested area when Riley yelped behind him.

'What is it?' asked Robert, alarmed. Riley practically jumped into his arms, pointing to a nearby swamp.

It looked as if the water was moving slowly. A moment later a large scaly head emerged, then ducked under again and drifted further away from the fascinated boys.

Robert pressed record on his voice recorder, a little breathless with excitement. 'I think Riley has just found our first prehistoric creature, and I reckon it's an *Archelon* (are-kell-on), a turtle that lived during the late Cretaceous period in North America.'

Riley took a closer look. 'That is one enormous turtle!'

Robert nodded. 'These guys can reach 3.6 metres in length – much bigger than any turtle humans have ever seen. And what's interesting is that they evolved to have a shell on their back. During the Cretaceous period, all they had was a tough leathery hide rather than a shell.'

Riley was impressed. 'This prehistoric stuff is much more interesting when you can actually see the creature you're talking about.'

'Let's keep moving,' said Robert. 'It's swampy around here, so be extra –'

There was a strange swallowing noise from behind Robert. He turned to see a speechless Riley disappearing from sight, as though the ground was swallowing him whole!

# CHAPTER FOUR

'Get me out of here!' Riley managed to gasp, as he quickly sank to waist height in swampy sand.

'Okay, don't panic.' Robert spun around, looking for a vine or branch that he could use.

'Too late! Get me out of here!' Riley

grabbed helplessly at some reeds, but they slipped through his fingers.

Robert ran to a shrub that had woody vines draped all over it. With a sharp tug, he disentangled one and hurried back to his friend. 'Tie the end around your waist. Hurry!'

Riley wasted no time arguing. This was a matter of life or death. He wrapped the woody vine around his torso, and held tightly to the knot as Robert wound the other end round and round his left wrist, and started pulling slowly.

'It's working!' yelled Riley excitedly,

as he felt himself getting pulled from the sandy claws of the quicksand.

Robert wasn't about to mention this to Riley, but he was a little worried about making a lot of noise just in case it drew unwanted attention. He wasn't sure how well theropods could hear, but he figured the sound of a 9-year-old boy shouting his lungs out in the middle of a swamp could travel for miles.

Finally, with lots of effort by Robert and energetic yelling and wriggling by Riley, they got Riley out. He was a bit of a mess, and the humidity in the air

meant that both boys were damp with sweat.

'Phew, that was a surprise,' said Robert, unravelling the woody vine from his arm and discarding it.

Riley was shaken. 'I was looking out for carnivores, not for quicksand.'

Robert helped dust his friend off. 'Let's head towards the forested area. Hopefully it'll be less swampy there. Follow in my footsteps.'

They walked carefully for a few hundred metres, and once they reached the forest's edge, the natural sunlight

was blocked, making everything a little darker and scarier.

Robert kept talking quietly to Riley, which helped to make them both feel less afraid. 'Apart from the turtles and other marine creatures, there are probably frogs and even small marsupials around here too. Keep your eyes peeled.'

Riley's eyes flickered from forest floor to treetops, taking it all in. 'I never thought I'd be saying this, but isn't it time we saw a dinosaur?'

Robert laughed. 'I was thinking the same thing, mate.'

A breathy whine floating through the trees interrupted the conversation.

Riley stopped. 'What was that?'

'I'm not sure.' Robert frowned.

They listened again. There was another whine.

'Let's go and investigate!' whispered Robert, his eyes sparkling with excitement, as they headed towards the mysterious noise.

# CHAPTER FIVE

The whines turned into grunts as the boys edged closer. Finally Robert and Riley got close enough to see the source of the unusual sound.

'Hey, look. Two army tanks,' whispered Riley.

There were two heavily plated

ankylosaurs at the base of a large redwood tree.

Robert was almost jumping up and down. 'They're *euoplocephaluses*, Riley. Incredible!' He grabbed his voice recorder once more. 'So we're in a deeply forested area and we've come across two *euoplocephaluses*. They're enormous, much bigger than I would've imagined, around 6 metres long, and one of them is using its duck-billed beak to chew on a shrub.'

Riley pointed to the second anklyo-saur. 'What's up with that guy?'

Robert continued his commentary. 'The second *euoplocephalus*, who is slightly smaller than his friend, seems to have tried to eat a vine that has tangled up one of his legs . . .'

The creature let out another breathy whine, similar to the one the boys had heard earlier.

'. . . and he's not happy about it. He's trying to chew through the vine, but it looks like the same kind of vine I used to help Riley out of the quicksand. Poor guy. It's going to take him a while to cut through that.' Robert pocketed his voice recorder.

The *euoplocephalus* was making the knot around his front leg worse, and was becoming more agitated. His companion didn't stop to help out, and instead was concentrating solely on chomping his own shrub. Obviously, in this environment, food came before friends.

'I'm glad they're not meat-eaters, Robert – they look tough!' said Riley, impressed.

Robert punched his friend on the arm. 'Exactly what I've been trying to say all day, mate. These guys are protective powerhouses. Just because they don't have the enormous jaws and teeth of the carnivore, doesn't mean they aren't awesome creatures.'

'Okay, well, I get what you were saying. Now I can see with my own eyes.' Riley shook his head. 'It is really amazing, isn't it?'

Robert smiled. 'I'm glad you're here to see it with me.'

All of a sudden, the larger *euoplocephalus* stopped eating, raised its head in the air and sniffed.

Riley looked worried. 'Do you think they can smell us?'

'I'm not sure.'

The smaller *euoplocephalus* was still busy fighting the vine.

After a second sniff, the free dinosaur started pawing the ground and let out a couple of snorts.

Meanwhile, the smaller *euoplocephalus* became more desperate, pawing and chewing the vine at the same time.

Robert was intrigued. 'This behaviour makes me think that the dinosaurs have sensed some kind of danger.'

Riley tensed. 'Then we should be getting away from here.'

'*Euoplocephaluses* have quite small brains, so it may be a false alarm.'

Riley looked at Robert incredulously. 'Mate, if there's a chance something with big teeth and an appetite is on its way here, I don't want to be the easy meal option.' He put on his carnivorous dinosaur voice. '"Hmmm, I could chew on a tough leathery dinosaur over there or go for the softer and tastier-looking human boy." Seriously, I'd know which meal I'd choose.'

Robert considered Riley's argument. 'Good point. Let's get off the ground.

But I want to keep an eye on this *euoplocephalus*, see if we can help him.'

As the boys found shelter, the larger *euoplocephalus* was now butting its buddy to get a move on.

The smaller 'saur was looking more and more frantic, but didn't seem to have the ability to untangle itself. Its companion sniffed the air once more and then took off, without a backwards glance, through a copse of trees.

The remaining *euoplocephalus* glanced after its departing friend, let out a whine and continued to struggle.

# CHAPTER SIX

It only took a moment for the predator to arrive. Riley had to stifle a cry. It did not look like the type of dinosaur you wanted to get too close to. 'What is it?' asked Riley, not sure if he really wanted to know the answer.

Robert stared at the creature in

amazement. 'I think it's a *Gorgosaurus* (gorr-goh-saw-russ).'

Riley shook his head. 'That's *another* dinosaur I've never heard of before.'

'It's very similar to *albertosaurus*,' Robert explained. 'It's a carnivore, and as you can see, its head is really large compared to the rest of its body. Smaller than *Tyrannosaurus rex* but just as deadly!'

As if responding to Robert's cue, the *gorgosaurus* opened its mouth and gave a bloodcurdling roar as he focused in on the *euoplocephalus*.

The *euoplocephalus* was trapped. Its tail was thrashing from side to side, but the persistent vine was not releasing its grip.

Robert started climbing down the tree.

'What are you doing?' whisper-shouted Riley. 'Are you crazy?'

Robert looked up at his friend, who was perched on a branch. 'Stay there, okay? I'm going to try to create a distraction.'

Before Riley could stop him, Robert scampered down to ground level and disappeared from sight. Riley's attention

turned back to the *gorgosaurus*. It was moving closer to the *euoplocephalus*, taking its time. There was no need to rush when dinner was tethered to a tree, waiting for you.

Riley couldn't bear to watch the armoured dinosaur get eaten. Even in the short time he'd seen him, he'd grown to like the tough creature.

In fact, Riley thought that if he were a dinosaur, he'd be like this guy. Sometimes, simple things like having a snack turned into unfortunate accidents for Riley too. He was just lucky he didn't

live in a time where an accident could involve getting eaten in one gulp by a hungry *gorgosaurus*.

With this realisation, Riley decided he wasn't going to stay in the tree either. He'd do what he could to help this dinosaur survive. Riley started climbing down the tree, but only a couple of branches down he lost his footing, falling the last couple of metres.

And in true Riley fashion – he couldn't help himself, after all – his *AAAARRRRGGGHHH* could be heard resounding throughout the Cretaceous period.

55

Robert was collecting large stones from a rocky area a few metres away from the drama when Riley's yell alerted him. His plan had been to throw as many rocks as possible into a nearby fern, hopefully attracting the attention of the *gorgosaurus* and giving the ankylosaur more time to break free. But he realised Riley's outburst might prove a more successful distraction . . . albeit a deadly one.

He kept a couple of the stones and

ran back to the tree where he'd left Riley behind. Riley was no longer there and neither was the *gorgosaurus*.

Oh no. Something had just gone very, very wrong!

# CHAPTER SEVEN

'Ri-ley!' shouted Robert, trying desperately to track down his friend.

There was no answer.

The trapped *euoplocephalus* looked over at the human boy in amazement. The poor ankylosaur had no idea what was going on. He whinnied in confusion.

Robert was worried for his friend, but he also knew that Riley had nine lives. Considering the amount of times his friend had got himself into death-defying trouble, he'd always managed to get out alive.

In a snap decision, Robert jogged over to the *euoplocephalus*, avoiding the club tail, which had started swinging in agitation. 'G'day, mate, my name's Robert,' he said quietly and calmly to the dinosaur. 'You've got yourself in a bind. Let me help.'

Of course the ankylosaur didn't know

what Robert was saying, but the soothing tone got the message across. It's tail stopped swinging.

Robert knew this was dangerous. There were spikes all over this dinosaur that could seriously hurt him. He grabbed hold of the woody vine wrapped tightly around the *euoplocephalus's* leg and, as quickly as he could, began to unwind it.

He spoke as he worked. 'This vine is fantastic for helping a friend out of quicksand, but I'd stay away from it as a food source. Okay?'

Using one of the stones he'd kept with him, Robert managed to cut the twisted vine with repeated blows. He pulled the last of the vine away from the *euoplocephalus's* foot, and discovered the end had got caught behind one of the armoured plates on its neck.

Finally the dinosaur was able to lift its released leg and back away, but the vine that was still attached to its neck stopped it from going any further.

'Let me finish. I'll have you free in a moment.' Robert grabbed the vine and pulled hard, finally dislodging it. 'There.

I've done it. You're dismissed, soldier.' He watched as the *euoplocephalus* moved its neck, sniffed the air, turned and then ran down the track into the forest.

Robert looked around him. The ferns rustled quietly in the gentle breeze. If it weren't for his friend having disappeared into thin air alongside a carnivorous dinosaur, he would have enjoyed the peaceful scene a lot more.

'Ri-ley!' Robert called out.

All of a sudden he could hear some-one, or something, running through the forest. But the acoustics were strange,

and he couldn't tell which direction the sound was coming from.

From the bush behind him came an explosion. Riley appeared, red-faced and wide-eyed. 'Run, mate, run!'

# CHAPTER EIGHT

Robert didn't need to be told twice. He ran, and from the snorting, huffing sound behind him, realised that the hungry *gorgosaurus* was in hot pursuit! He wasn't sure how long the carnivore had been chasing Riley, but he was impressed his friend had survived this long!

The boys got whipped in the face with fern fronds and the odd vine as they sprinted through the forest, but they didn't waste precious breath complaining about it. They dodged rocks, stones, branches and a couple of unnamed large rodents, which promptly scattered when they saw what was after the boys.

'What made you think outrunning a *gorgosaurus* was a good idea?' asked Robert, as they jumped over a small stream.

Riley wheezed before replying, 'I didn't want to see the armoured tank go down.'

Robert grinned at his friend. 'I got him loose in the end. You probably saved his life, you know.'

'You can call me Riley Harper, Dinosaur Rescuer, from now on,' puffed Riley, and the duo ducked around another ferny area.

'I'll be calling you Riley Harper, Dinosaur *Food,* if we don't get this *gorgosaurus* off our tail soon!' quipped Robert.

The *gorgosaurus* steadfastly refused to give up. It had walked away from an easy dinner, and was not going to stop running until it tried this unusual species ahead. There was a bonus too. If the first one tasted good, there were seconds not far behind!

After sidestepping around a particularly large tree trunk, the boys screeched to a stop near the edge of a rocky outcrop.

*Whoooaa!*

Below them was a sheer drop of at least 15 metres. There was nowhere else to run.

The boys turned around to see the *gorgosaurus* also grind to a halt, wearing a victor's large-toothed smile.

Robert turned to Riley. He was puffing so hard he had trouble speaking. 'Riley, mate, sorry about this.'

Riley was gulping in breaths. 'Would be good to have some . . . great defensive tactic to use right now.'

Robert sighed. 'Copy that, soldier.'

At that moment thunder struck, which was surprising because it was a nice sunny day without a cloud to be seen. Confused, the *gorgosaurus* and the boys looked up at the sky.

# CHAPTER NINE

The two boys glanced at each other, then at the sky again, then at the gorgosaurus, who seemed just as confused as the boys.

All of a sudden the thundering got closer, and four tank-like *euoplocephaluses*, trampling over ferns and other shrubs, appeared at the forest's

edge. They stopped in one defensive line, heads down, spikes gleaming, as though they were answering the call of an army general.

Robert noted that the smaller 'saur on the edge of the line was the one he'd rescued earlier. He allowed himself a grin. 'I think our backup troops have arrived.'

Riley's eyes were as big as saucers. 'How is this going to play out?'

Robert shrugged. 'Let's wait and see.' He looked behind him, down at the 15-metre drop. 'We have nowhere else to go.'

The *gorgosaurus* was also considering its options. It could take on a smaller *euoplocephalus* tangled up in a vine, but four creatures, appearing as though they were ready for serious action, were a force to be reckoned with.

The *gorgosaurus* let out an angry roar. But the *euoplocephaluses* stood their ground, refusing to budge.

The *gorgosaurus* roared once more, in a 'this is just not my lucky day' sort of way, and daintily moved to the edge of the line of ankylosaurs before bolting back into the forest.

Riley and Robert started clapping and cheering. 'Awesome work, guys!'

The *euoplocephaluses* lifted their heads, turned around and trundled back into the forest.

Robert and Riley saluted as the dinosaurs retreated.

'Enough adventure for today?' asked Robert with a tired grin.

'Well, I'm growing to like the place, but unless we can get a vegemite sandwich around here,' joked Riley, 'we have to go back.'

Robert considered the possibility.

'I'm not sure what year vegemite was invented, but I think it probably wasn't 70 million years ago.'

Riley nodded seriously. 'Probably not.' He glanced around. 'So how do we leave this place?'

'I think we need water,' said Robert. 'Let's head back to that swampy area across the forest.'

'Copy that, soldier,' said Riley, and the two boys strode off, marching in formation.

# CHAPTER TEN

The two friends had an uneventful trip back through the forest.

While Robert used the time to record what had happened between the *gorgosaurus* and the *euoplocephaluses*, Riley tried to avoid falling into more quicksand or getting chased by a carnivore.

He did narrowly miss getting bitten by what looked like a prehistoric mosquito, though it wasn't the size of a modern-day mozzie. It was about a hundred times bigger. Riley used a fern frond to bat the creature out of his path and watched it hit a nearby tree trunk with a satisfying thud.

Normally this would've been big news, but after what had already happened today, a prehistoric, monster-sized mozzie was not even worth mentioning.

When the boys finally reached the swamp, Robert got out the fossil and

the two friends splashed water on each other . . . and nothing happened.

Robert sighed. 'I think we might have to jump in.'

Riley did a quick check to make sure the swamp wasn't harbouring any archelon or plesiosaurs, and announced, 'Last one in's a rotten egg!' Then he grabbed his friend and together they dive-bombed into the water.

Robert and Riley felt intensely wet, then dizzy, then wet again, and then as though they were falling through a tornado during a storm.

Arriving back by their tranquil camp site moments later, the boys were sprawled in a wet heap. Robert felt the compact weight of the digital voice recorder in his pocket as he got up. 'Good thing it's waterproof,' he thought.

Uncle Nate reappeared with two bottles of drinking water, and gave the boys a curious once-over. 'Okay then. You decided to swim in the lake . . . with your clothes on.' He shrugged. 'Why not?' He handed the two boys a bottle of water each. 'Cheers.'

Later that evening, Uncle Nate and the two boys were sleeping peacefully. The sound of a great horned owl could be heard in the distance.

*Ho hoo hoo hoododo. Ho hoo hoo hoododo.*

Suddenly Riley sat bolt upright, arms flailing, screaming, 'Get the *gorgosaurus* off me!'

Uncle Nate and Robert jerked awake, startled by the outburst.

'What did you say, little guy?' asked a bleary-eyed Uncle Nate.

Riley looked around, realising he'd been dreaming. 'Oh, ummm, nothing.'

Uncle Nate glanced over at him. 'You were dreaming of being eaten by a what? A *gorgosaurus*?'

Riley was a little embarrassed. 'Sort of.'

Robert came to his friend's rescue. 'That's strange, because I'd been dreaming about an *albertosaurus* climbing into the station wagon while we were stopped at traffic lights.'

Uncle Nate seemed bewildered. 'You boys have extremely imaginative

84

dreams. But I guess that as long as your waking life isn't dangerous, there's no harm done.' He lay back on his pillow and was snoring softly seconds later.

Riley and Robert shared a look.

'Sleep well, mate,' yawned Robert.

Riley grinned. 'Don't let the bedbugs bite.'

Robert looked serious. 'It's actually the scorpions you have to be careful of around here.'

Riley jerked back upright, eyes wide in alarm, as Robert snuggled into his sleeping bag, chuckling to himself.

Drawn by Robert Irwin

# EUOPLOCEPHALUS

**ALSO KNOWN AS:** Dyoplosaurus

**DISCOVERED:** 1902 in Alberta, Canada

**ETYMOLOGY:** Well-armoured head

**PERIOD:** Late Cretaceous period, 70–65 million years ago

**LENGTH:** Approximately 6 metres long

**HEIGHT:** Approximately 1.8 metres tall

**WEIGHT:** Approximately 2 tonnes

*Euoplocephaluses* were herbivores that thrived towards the end of the Cretaceous period. They were built like military tanks, and some species were about the same size. Massive hips and legs supported their heavy bodies. They had thick plates and spikes on their backs, but the armour on their heads was much more developed. They also had a unique weapon — a large ball of bone at the end of their tail, which could be swung from side to side like a club.

*Euoplocephalus's* head was a heavy bot of bone, covered in thick plates. Thick spines protected the sides of its face, and even its eyelids were armoured.

There was a horny, toothless beak at the front of its wide face.

*Euoplocephalus* was discovered in 1902

by Lawrence Lambe, who proposed the name 'stereocephalus'. However, this term was already being used for an insect, so the name of the dinosaur was changed to *euoplocephalus* in 1910.

Two species of *euoplocephaluses* are known to have existed: the original species, *Euoplocephalus tutus*, and a second species, *Euoplocephalus acutosquameus*, which was discovered in 1924 by William Arthur Parks. The species have different shaped clubs in their tails, but despite this, some scientists believe they are in fact a single species.

*Euoplocephalus* is the best-known ankylosaur among paleontologists, with the discovery of over 40 more-or-less complete skeletons (including about 15 intact skulls). However, since the remains of multiple *euoplocephaluses* have never been found heaped together, it's likely that this herbivore led a solitary lifestyle, though some experts believe *euoplocephalus* may have roamed the North American plains in small herds.

# THE CANADIAN BADLANDS

This region in Alberta, Canada is famous for rich deposits of fossils, including dinosaur bones, which can be seen at the UNESCO World Heritage Site Dinosaur Provincial Park, and are displayed at the Royal Tyrrell Museum.

Dinosaur Provincial Park is located in the heart of the province of Alberta's badlands and contains some of the most important fossil discoveries ever made from the Age of Reptiles, in particular about 35 species of dinosaur that date back 75 million years.

More than 300 dinosaur skeletons have been pulled from a 27-kilometre stretch along the Red Deer River since digging began there in the 1880s, and dozens of these now grace museums in 30 cities around the world. Since 1985 the largest collection of treasures from the park has been housed in the Royal Tyrrell Museum of Palaeontology in Drumheller, Canada.

# THE DINOSAUR FEATHER

## WRITTEN BY JACK WELLS

RANDOM HOUSE AUSTRALIA

# CHAPTER ONE

The humid Queensland air stuck to Robert's face like vegemite at lunchtime. Gently, he pulled back the fern he was hiding behind. He wanted to get a better look at the creature.

'She's a real beauty,' he whispered. 'Almost 2 metres tall and pretty heavy.

Believe it or not, these wonderful animals can run up to 50 kilometres an hour. They can jump and swim too.'

He squatted down but stretched his neck over the plant's soft, leafy fronds.

'Usually they are shy, solitary creatures,' he said, 'but when they're frightened, you'd better watch out! The name we gave this one says it all: Stomp!'

It was then that Robert leant too heavily on the light branch he was holding. He lost his balance and fell forwards into the moist and dirty leaf

litter, hitting the ground with a *thud*. Someone laughed from a short distance away and a startled Stomp the cassowary dashed off into the scrub.

'Cut!' said the director.

The camera operator and sound recordist sighed and lowered their heavy equipment.

Robert turned to his best friend. 'Crikey, Riley,' he said, getting to his feet, 'you have to be quiet. It could take ages to find Stomp again.'

'No way,' said Riley. 'Those birds are massive.'

Robert began brushing dirt and wet leaves off his khaki pants and shirt. 'But they're really shy.'

'Oh, sorry,' chuckled Riley. 'I couldn't help it. You should have seen your face when you fell. It was hilarious.'

The two friends smiled. Robert could never stay cross at Riley for long. He told himself for the millionth time how lucky he was to live at Australia Zoo and tell visitors about cassowaries and the other amazing animals that lived there.

Robert's mother Terri and older sister Bindi walked over from where they had

been watching the film shoot. 'Great job, Robert,' said his mum, 'but stop beating up on the tree ferns!' She gave him a warm smile. 'I can see you'll be as great on TV as your father.'

'And your sister!' said Bindi, tickling her little brother around his waist.

Now it was Robert's turn to laugh.

'So, have we finished bird-watching now?' asked Riley. 'I want to go see the crocs!'

Terri chuckled. 'You and Robert are becoming more similar every day. Like two birds of a feather.'

Robert and Riley grinned. They both knew Terri was right.

Simon, who had been directing the film shoot, asked them not to go see the crocs just yet. 'We need to find Stomp again,' he said. 'I have to wrap this shoot today.'

Riley didn't like hearing that. His moan sounded like a roar from one of Australia Zoo's tigers.

'That was awesome, Robert,' Simon said. 'You made the cassowary seem so exciting. It was almost like you were talking about a dinosaur or something.'

Robert's eyes widened. Dinosaurs were his special subject. He was an expert, and one day he hoped to become a palaeontologist. 'It's funny you say that,' he said. 'Birds and dinosaurs have more in common than most people think.'

Simon smiled. 'I'd heard that they call you the Dinosaur Hunter.'

Robert and Riley shared a smile. No-one but the two of them knew just how truthful that name had become.

As it was time for Bindi and Terri to help the keepers feed Graham, their giant crocodile, the camera crew

decided to sit in the shade for a 10-minute break.

'Can I go too?' whined Riley.

'We'll meet you at the crocs when you've finished filming,' Bindi answered.

Robert slapped his friend on the back. 'Looks like you're stuck here with me,' he said.

Riley sighed. 'I suppose the crocs won't be going anywhere. Besides, cassowaries are pretty cool too, really.'

Robert nodded in agreement, thinking of the bird's dark black feathers and its bright red and blue decoration.

'They are the third largest bird in the world,' said Robert. 'Only the ostrich and emu are taller.'

Riley picked up a large, flat piece of bark and held it to his head like a shark fin. 'What are those horn things on their heads for?'

Robert grinned. 'They're called *casques*. We're not sure, but they could be for display, protection or even to help cassowaries make their distinctive super-low calls.'

Suddenly, a low, booming sound came from a short distance away within some

trees. Robert and Riley spun around and looked at each other.

'Stomp!' they cried.

# CHAPTER TWO

The two boys dashed swiftly but quietly through the dense tree area of Australia Zoo. They didn't hear any more cassowary calls, just the high-pitched tweeting and honking of the other birds in the treetops above.

Then there was a rustle in the bushes

a few metres in front of them. Robert motioned to his friend to get down low.

'Is that a cassowary?' squawked Riley.

'Ssh!' said Robert.

Everyone in the Irwin family was good at handling and studying animals, and Robert was no different. He knew that any sudden movements or sounds could frighten away whatever was foraging in the bushes.

They both lay silently on the ground, watching the plants in front of them, waiting for the animal to show itself.

Lying on the ground, Robert could feel his prized possession in his shorts pocket – the fossilised *australovenator* (*oss-tra-low-ven-ah-tor*) claw he always carried with him. He had unearthed it on a fossil dig on his last birthday. Somehow, the claw had managed to transport Robert and Riley back in time to the Age of Dinosaurs. Robert smiled, thinking of all the mind-blowing adventures he'd already had.

Then the familiar long neck of Stomp the cassowary appeared between some plants.

'It's her, all right,' whispered Robert.

'What's she doing?' hissed Riley.

'She's looking for fallen fruit,' said Robert as quietly as he could. 'Cassowaries are mostly frugivorous. That means fruit is their main source of food.'

Stomp found something particularly delicious not far from the boys. They watched her enjoy it before Robert continued. 'Humans have made cassowaries an endangered species by destroying their habitats,' he said. 'The

sad thing is, if cassowaries die out, many of the plants in our rainforests will too. Cassowaries help spread their seeds around.'

Riley looked quizzically at Robert. 'How can they do that?' he asked. 'They don't have hands.'

Then Stomp passed a large amount of droppings as she walked in front of their hiding spot.

'That's how,' said Robert.

Riley gave such a disgusted look that Robert had to fight the urge to laugh out loud. 'Come on,' he chuckled. 'We

should get the others and try filming again.'

But Riley didn't move. He was in awe of the bird that was larger than him. 'They're definitely big,' he said. 'Imagine how huge their eggs must be!'

'They're about 14 centimetres long, I think,' said Robert. 'Actually, that would be about the same size as some dinosaur eggs.'

'That reminds me, what were you saying before?' asked Riley. 'I mean, birds and dinosaurs can't really be related, can they?'

'Why not?'

'I know cassowaries are big, but dinosaurs were so much bigger.'

'Many dinosaurs were smaller than cassowaries,' said Robert. *'Micropachycephalosaurus (micro-packy-sef-a-lo-sor-us)* was just over half a metre long. They're one of my favourites. They probably would have even been afraid of our Stomp!'

Riley laughed. 'Micro-*what*-a-saurus? That's a long name for a small dinosaur!'

'I reckon!' Robert smiled. 'It took lots of practice to learn how to say it properly.'

'But I've seen dinosaurs,' said Riley, 'and they look totally different to birds. Dinosaurs didn't have wings or beaks. They didn't even have feathers!'

'Many dinosaurs did have feathers,' said Robert. 'Some had wings, and some had toothless mouths like beaks.'

Stomp was now scratching in the dirt. Her three-toed feet were fearsome to watch in action, especially the long, middle claw on each one.

'There are other similarities too,' said Robert. 'Where else have you seen a claw like that?'

'Your *australovenator* claw!' squealed Riley. 'Quick, pull it out – I want to see how it measures up to Stomp's.'

Carefully, Robert slid the claw out of his pocket and held it in front of his face. He lined it up in his vision with the cassowary's claws.

'Let me see,' said Riley. He reached out for the claw, bumping Robert's arm.

'Careful,' whispered Robert, 'it's millions of years old. I don't want to drop it.'

Riley swiped at the claw. His fingers

grabbed at it, clenching both the claw and Robert's hand at the same time.

'Ow! Riley!'

As the claw pricked Robert's palm, he knew his shout had scared Stomp away. He looked up to see the tall cassowary disappear . . . and then everything else did as well. The trees, sky and ground went all wobbly, then vanished and changed. Dizziness took over and the two boys couldn't tell which way was up.

# CHAPTER THREE

When Robert opened his eyes, he and Riley were still lying on the ground, surrounded by trees. Nothing much had changed.

Then Riley spoke. 'Is it just me or did it get a little chilly all of a sudden?'

It had. A moment ago Robert had been sweating in the heat. 'Yes,' said

Robert, blowing air into his hands. 'And look, these plants aren't the kinds we have at home.'

'This isn't Australia Zoo any more, is it?' asked Riley.

Robert shook his head. His claw had surely transported them to another prehistoric dinosaur habitat. 'I wonder where we are, though. And when!'

They stood up and walked cautiously through the thinly forested area, rubbing their bare arms to try to warm up. Now they weren't worried about staying hidden from cassowaries. From experience, they thought carnivorous dinosaurs might be the real threat here.

They scanned their surroundings for anything dangerous as they walked. After a minute or two, Robert held up his hand. 'Stop,' he whispered. 'Look in the clearing over there.'

Riley squinted into the distance. 'Dinosaurs!' he said.

'Right,' said Robert. 'A *Segnosaur* (seg-no-sore)! That means only one thing.' He placed the magic claw back into his shorts pocket and pulled out the other object he never left home

without – his digital voice recorder. Robert quickly pressed record. 'We have arrived in the late Cretaceous period, maybe 75 million years ago. Some *segnosaurs* are drinking from a stream in the distance. That means we are probably somewhere in Central Asia.'

Somehow the claw had taken them to a whole new continent!

'Awesome,' said Riley. 'But it's just like I told you – dinosaurs don't have feathers or wings. Even from this distance I can see that.'

Robert squinted to see the reptiles better in the glare of the midday sun.

'Birds are thought to have evolved from theropods, not *segnosaurs*.'

'Do you think we might meet some theropods or feathered dinosaurs here?'

'There's a good chance,' said Robert. 'Most of the fossils found of feathered dinosaurs have been uncovered in China.'

A couple of *segnosaurs* had stopped lapping at the stream and were beginning to walk away on their four powerful limbs. They reminded Robert of the big crocs back home that Riley had been so desperate to see. 'It's funny,' he said, 'scientists now know that *Tyrannosaurus rex* had just as much in common with birds as with reptiles like crocs or alligators.'

Riley shook his head. 'I don't know, mate,' he said. 'You're my best friend and you know so much more about animals than I do, but I'm not sure if I'll believe that until I see it for myself.'

'Fair enough,' replied Robert.

'Look around you,' continued Riley. 'There are no feathered dinosaurs, just the *segnosaurs* and that giant bird sitting in its nest over there.'

Robert's ears tingled. 'Giant bird?' he echoed. 'Where?'

Riley pointed back in the direction they had come. 'See? It's sitting in a nest among all the trees.'

'But, Riley,' shouted Robert as he jumped around excitedly, 'that isn't a bird!'

'What are you talking about?'

Robert placed his voice recorder close to his mouth. 'Riley has just pointed out an *Oviraptor* (o-vee-rap-tor) sitting in its nest,' he said slowly. 'A dinosaur completely covered in colourful feathers!'

# CHAPTER FOUR

Riley gasped. 'Crikey!'

'You took the words right out of my mouth,' said Robert. 'This is awesome!'

The two boys walked back towards the *oviraptor*. As they got closer, they crept on all fours, trying to get as near to the dinosaur as they dared.

The dinosaur was sitting in a large nest on the ground, spreading its feathered arms over its eggs for protection. Robert had to admit the arms looked a lot like wings. He had to keep reminding himself that *oviraptors* were dinosaurs – reptiles – and not birds.

They stopped and tried to get a better look through the plants that surrounded the *oviraptor*. 'This is close enough,' said Robert.

Riley agreed. 'I don't need her thinking we're after her eggs.'

Robert studied the *oviraptor*. 'To tell you the truth, I don't know if that's a she or a he.'

Riley shot his friend a confused glance. 'What do you mean? She's a mum sitting in her nest!'

'But rules aren't strict in the animal world,' said Robert. 'I mean, with cassowaries, it's the male who looks after the eggs and the chicks.'

Riley put his hands on his hips. 'Am I going crazy? Dinosaurs that look like birds, dads acting like mums. What's next? Fish running a marathon?'

Robert laughed. 'Just keep your voice down. Whether it's a male or female *oviraptor*, I don't want to bother it!'

Riley continued rubbing his cold arms while Robert spoke into his recorder again. 'The *oviraptor's* arms are short and feathered. We can't see the tail. I hope to see it feed with its powerful beak while we're here.'

'I was sure it was a bird,' whispered Riley. 'It isn't as big as other dinosaurs. It isn't even as big as a cassowary. And it has that thing on its head like cassowaries do too.'

Robert spied another glance at the *oviraptor*. Riley was right. How had he not noticed the dome on its head before? The similarities between the two animals were amazing, even though one was a reptile, the other a bird, and they lived 75 million years apart!

The *oviraptor* buried its head under an arm to take a snooze. Robert and Riley just stared at it, almost in the open now, less worried of being noticed. They warmed their hands in their pockets as they watched.

'I guess the feathers keep them warm,'

said Robert. 'I'm sure the *oviraptor* isn't feeling the cold like we are.'

'True.'

'Lots of dinosaurs had feathers,' Robert continued. '*Khaan*, *mononykus*, and one of my favourites: the beautiful *caudipteryx*.'

'Fine,' sighed Riley, 'but I know none of the famous dinosaurs like *velociraptor* or *tyrannosaurus* had feathers.'

Robert raised an eyebrow but said nothing.

Riley stopped. 'No way!' he cried.

'Yep! *Tyrannosaurus* and *velociraptor* are both believed to have had feathers.'

Robert laughed. 'At least on some parts of their bodies, or when they were babies.'

'I don't believe this!' shouted Riley. 'I get whizzed back in time, there are feathered dinosaurs, it's freezing, and – and – *aa-choo!*'

'Now the *oviraptor* is staring at us!' said Robert, alarmed. 'Quick, let's get out of here!'

# CHAPTER FIVE

But they couldn't run. Their feet were frozen, and it wasn't just because it was cold. Partly through fear, partly in amazement, the two boys stood like statues and stared at the *oviraptor* as it raised itself up on its two long legs.

'Look,' said Robert, pointing at the tip

of the *oviraptor's* tail. 'There's another reason for having feathers: presentation.'

The *oviraptor* fanned out the beautiful, long feathers on the tip of its tail, almost like a peacock might do. Then it made a loud squealy, squawky sound that echoed all around them.

'That's all the presentation I need to see,' said Riley. 'I'm out of here!'

Riley turned and ran into the cover of the denser trees behind them. Robert was quick to follow, but in the back of his mind he knew they could never outrun an *oviraptor*.

Robert kept looking back as they skipped over tree roots and plants. The *oviraptor* was only about as tall as they were, but it had a sharp beak and claws.

The dinosaur ran after them for a little way, but then stopped, seemingly happy to see the egg thieves scared off.

Robert called out to his friend to stop running, but Riley didn't until he had found protection behind a large tree.

He was breathing heavily as Robert ran around to join him. They stood for a moment, leaning on the trunk and catching their breath. Robert saw they were at the top of a hill. It was quite steep and he couldn't see the bottom, thanks to the small plants and trees that grew all over it.

Once he'd caught his breath, he took out his voice recorder. 'The *oviraptor* was very protective of its nest,' said Robert into the microphone. 'We will do our best to stay clear of any more of them.'

Then he looked down. Lying at the foot of the tree, between two roots, was a round, smooth and lightly coloured object. 'Hey, Riley, look!' he said.

'Whoa! Is that an egg? A dinosaur egg?'

Robert picked it up gently and turned to face Riley. 'It's big but not gigantic. I can hold it in my palm,' he said. 'I wonder if it's from an *oviraptor's* nest?'

'But what's it doing here?'

Their breathing quickened again, this time from excitement. They knew how lucky they were to be holding an actual prehistoric egg. 'I don't know,' said Robert, cradling the egg in his palm, 'but its home must be close by.'

Robert and Riley looked at each other. They both knew the egg might have been

41

lying there for days, but they couldn't just leave it.

'If it *is* the *oviraptor's* egg,' said Riley, 'I'm not going back there. I don't want to be screeched at again. I'm not a fan of running for my life!'

'At least it warmed us up a bit,' said Robert with a smile.

'Being warm is nice, but being safe is better,' said Riley.

'Mate, there's nothing to worry about,' reassured Robert. 'We'll just creep back towards the nest and wait in hiding for a glimpse of the eggs. If they match, we'll

slip it in while the *oviraptor* sleeps.'

Riley was still leaning with his back and hands on the tree, looking down the steep hill. 'You're sure we'll be safe?'

'Yes.' Robert nodded. 'Just don't sneeze this time.'

Just then an *oviraptor* reappeared from around the tree, opened its beak and squealed at full volume in Robert's face.

Robert jumped, almost dropping the egg. Riley screamed in terror before stepping away from the tree, tripping on some roots and rolling down the long, dirty hill.

# CHAPTER SIX

'Aaah! Robert!' cried Riley as he rolled
away. 'Save me!'

Riley's shouting startled the beautiful
but fierce *oviraptor*. It shrieked and ran
away, leaving Robert alone but shaken.

He held the egg in both hands like a
priceless gem and approached the top

45

of the hill. Looking down, he couldn't see Riley any more, though the constant yelping told Robert that his friend was scared but unhurt.

'Don't worry, mate,' Robert's voice echoed into the valley, 'I'm coming!'

Robert made his way down the hill with sideways steps, ensuring his boots were firmly placed before taking each step. If he tripped, not only might he get hurt, but the egg would probably be crushed.

In no time at all, Robert was most of the way down and leaning on a thin tree.

From there he could see Riley, who had stopped rolling and was sitting at the bottom of the hill. 'Stay there, I'm on my way,' Robert called.

Riley looked up the slope and gave Robert the 'okay' sign. 'I guess that was one way to escape a protective *oviraptor*,' he chuckled as he patted his legs clean.

But Robert didn't come. He was pointing over Riley's shoulder in alarm.

'What's wrong?' puzzled Riley. He turned and stared straight into the eyes of another wild *oviraptor*.

47

Riley turned and began clambering back up the hill on all fours. Dirt flew everywhere. A dust cloud covered the *oviraptor's* densely feathered body. It swiped its domed head at Riley's legs as he crawled up the hill, but missed.

Robert laid the egg on the ground within a large, fallen leaf. He stretched an arm down towards Riley while holding onto the trunk of the thin tree. As soon as Riley was close enough, Robert grabbed his hand and pulled him up behind the tree. The *oviraptor* gave out a shrill call from below.

'I think I've seen enough feathered dinosaurs to last me a lifetime,' said Riley, panting hard.

'It's okay,' said Robert. 'It won't be following you up. Look!'

A small group of two-legged dino-saurs emerged from within the trees at the base of the hill and approached the *oviraptor*. These dinosaurs were similar in size to the *oviraptor* but they didn't have feathers. They hissed at the *oviraptor*, who squealed back at them before deciding to leave the newcomers in peace.

'Please tell me these ones won't eat us,' said Riley, watching from above.

'They won't. They're herbivores,' said Robert.

Riley sat down in relief. 'What kind of dinosaurs are they?' he asked. 'I owe those little guys my thanks.'

'I think they're *micropachycephalosauruses*,' said Robert, excitedly.

'Of course, the dinosaurs with the name longer than they are,' said Riley. 'But today is Topsy-turvy Day so why should I be surprised?'

# CHAPTER SEVEN

The two young dinosaur hunters looked down from either side of the tree. Robert watched in awe as a group of one of his favourite ancient reptiles foraged for plants to eat.

He remembered the first time he had heard about the *micropachy-*

*cephalosaurus*. On his last birthday, while digging for fossils for the Australian Age of Dinosaurs museum, Robert had seen a drawing of one. Immediately after realising he would have been taller than a *micropachycephalosaurus*, it became one of Robert's favourite dinosaurs. After all, he had already fed crocodiles longer than they were! As interesting as cassowaries were, filming a video about a metre-long *micropachycephalosaurus* at Australia Zoo was Robert's dream.

'It's funny that we're on a hill,' said Robert.

'It's not that funny if you roll down it,' said Riley, rubbing his leg.

'No, I mean the first *micropachy-cephalosaurus* fossil was found in China on a cliff.' Robert paused and turned to his friend. 'Maybe this is the place.'

Robert's fingers stretched across the shell of the smooth egg that was now safely back in his hands. He wanted to keep it warm in the hope of saving any baby dinosaur that may be growing inside. Watching the small dinosaurs, Robert wondered if the egg might belong to one of them.

'Riley, have you seen any dinosaur nests around here?' he asked.

Riley took his eyes off the dinosaurs for a moment. 'No, why?'

'I'm just trying to figure out who owns this egg.' Robert held the egg carefully in one hand as he pulled out his voice recorder. 'We have discovered a small pack of *micropachycephalosauruses*,' he said. 'Probably a family group. They are eating leaves off smaller plants. They are definitely shorter than *oviraptors*. I reckon they could run pretty fast.'

'Speaking of running,' said Riley, 'here they come!'

Some of the small dinosaurs were coming up the hill and towards the boys to try a clump of fresh leaves growing on a nearby plant.

Riley looked a little nervous. 'You're positive they aren't meat-eaters?' he asked again.

'Yeah,' said Robert. 'Watch, they prefer salad.'

Two *micropachycephalosauruses* were bickering over the leaves. They were now less than 5 metres from the boys. Robert was certain the dinosaurs must have been aware of their presence by now. Maybe they didn't mind being watched?

'They're amazing,' said Riley, 'but I'm starting to get cold again. Maybe we should try to get home.'

'Y-y-yeah –' said Robert.

The whole world was vibrating. Something large had fallen on the ground nearby, shaking the leaves in the tree above the boys' heads. Then the ground shook again, and again. Robert almost dropped the egg before whipping his other hand over the top of it for safety.

Suddenly, from somewhere in the valley below, came a shriek that made

the entire group of *micropachycephalo-sauruses* turn and run at full pace up the hill, past Robert and Riley.

Robert guessed that not too far away, a large meat-eater had just made lunch out of one of their brothers or sisters. And whatever enjoyed eating them probably wouldn't mind snacking on small humans either.

'We better run,' yelled Robert. 'Now!'

Riley didn't need any encouragement. He jumped down and started pumping his legs as fast as they could carry him up the hill. 'Whatever it is,' he panted, 'I hope it only wants to eat salad!'

# CHAPTER EIGHT

The boys knew they would feel safer on higher ground. The denser plants that they had found around the *oviraptor* nest would give them more of a chance to hide too. But running up the hill was a lot harder than rolling down it.

Whatever giant beast was approaching,

feeding on a *micropachycephalosaurus* hadn't slowed it down much. Robert and Riley felt each of its footfalls as they climbed higher.

'What do you think it is?' asked Riley. His cheeks were turning pink from the cold.

'I'm not sure,' said Robert, 'but judging from the vibrations we can feel, it's big.'

Robert and Riley stumbled a few times but slowly rose upwards. Whenever they got close to a plant or tree Riley would grab it to steady himself.

It was even harder for Robert, who had to climb without using his hands. He held the egg with a firm but gentle grip.

Finally, Robert's foot fell flat on the top of the hill. 'Quick, let's find a hiding place,' he wheezed.

'Look,' shouted Riley, 'there's the tree you found the egg under.' He was pointing to his right, which meant that to their left was where they first appeared in late Cretaceous Asia. The nesting *oviraptor* was in that direction too.

They ran straight ahead, under the cover of the trees and plants. Robert

looked up at the treetops as he ran, while Riley looked for any evidence of angry, nesting *oviraptors*.

'Find a good tree to climb,' said Robert. 'I want to have a better view of what's coming.'

Riley squealed. 'But the higher you are, the closer to the dinosaur's mouth you'll be!'

'Not necessarily,' said Robert, testing a foot on a strong branch. 'I'll only watch for a moment anyway. I just want to see what it is.'

As Robert searched, Riley stopped

and hugged himself for warmth. 'I just hope it doesn't come this way at all,' he said.

Robert ended up deciding on a tree at the top of the hill, next to the one they had found the egg under. It had regular, strong branches that would be easy to climb. It would also give him a good view of the valley.

Robert tucked his shirt into his pants and gently lowered the egg down his front. It felt warm against his stomach. Then he reached high for a branch and pulled himself up.

Soon Robert had climbed as high as he could go and Riley was looking up at him wide-eyed from about three metres below.

'Just be careful,' whispered Riley. 'Don't fall.'

Robert laughed. 'Don't worry, I don't really want dinosaur egg yolk down my pants!'

They didn't have long to wait. The sound of footsteps told Robert that the mystery dinosaur was coming closer.

With each passing second its footsteps grew louder. Robert's eyes

were glued to the treetops, waiting for a glimpse of the mystery dinosaur.

Robert could sense that the predator wasn't trying to walk up the hill, but was walking around it. A moment later, he got his first look at the head of the dinosaur. Next, Robert saw its neck, shoulders and arms as it climbed higher. 'Riley!' he shouted. 'Check it out!'

'No, I don't want to,' Riley called from the base of the tree. 'No way. I've had enough.' Riley hugged the tree trunk tightly and shut his eyes.

Suddenly, looking between the leaves

just to the right, Robert could see the entire creature from head to toe. It was now about 50 metres away, and on the same ground level as the boys. It seemed to be looking for something. 'Mate, you must see this!' Robert whispered to Riley.

He saw Riley open one eye just a crack as he clung to the tree like a koala. But once he had caught a glimpse of the 'saur, Riley swung around to get a proper look. 'Whoa!'

The dinosaur was large – perhaps 9 metres long. Its head was big too, with a small horn on its forehead and two large nostrils on top of its snout. The dinosaur yawned, showing long sharp teeth. It should have been one of the most fearsome reptiles the boys had ever seen, but the fact that it was covered from head to toe in long, thick feathers somehow made it seem more cuddly than scary.

'Is that a *tyrannosaurus rex*,' asked Riley, 'or the biggest bird of all time?'

Robert pictured a *tyrannosaurus* in his mind. This dinosaur was a bit smaller and its arms were longer, but Robert agreed it was very similar to a T-rex. It was then that he realised exactly what

it was. 'It's *tyrannosaurus's* cousin,' he said, looking down at Riley. 'It's called *Yutyrannus* (yu-ti-ran-us). The name means "feathered tyrant".'

Robert pulled his voice recorder out with his free hand. 'We're standing very close to a *yutyrannus*. Can you believe it?' he whispered. 'The largest dinosaur fossil ever found with visible feathers was one of them.'

The *yutyrannus* began walking again, towards them. The cold breeze picked up, making its feathers ripple like a wave rolling in at the beach.

Robert turned off the recorder. 'Uh-oh, I think we're about to have a visitor.'

Riley yelped. 'What! Make way, I'm coming up too,' he said, scrambling to climb the tree before the feathered tyrant could step on him.

# CHAPTER NINE

Riley joined Robert in the tree, standing one branch below him. 'Do you think it's coming to eat us?' he whispered.

'I'm not sure,' said Robert. 'I think it's looking for something.'

'Maybe it's lost an egg,' suggested Riley.

Robert felt the egg through his shirt. 'I don't think so,' he said. 'It's too little to be an egg laid by a dinosaur that size.'

The *yutyrannus* walked closer, brushing past branches and leaves as it came. Its face, with coloured, wavy feathers between its eyes, was heading straight for the boys. With each step, the feathered beast caused the tree to vibrate slightly. Soon, it was close enough that it could have reached out and knocked them down.

Then it stopped again. Robert's heart was beating so hard he could feel his

pulse in his hands as he gripped the tree. Riley was still and silent just below him.

The *yutyrannus* looked up and around. Whatever it was searching for was high off the ground. It turned, and Robert saw its long tail swing round. Robert could have reached out and touched it. He wondered what its long, bird-like feathers felt like.

But he couldn't risk it.

'I think it's leaving,' whispered Robert.

And then the *yutyrannus* jumped and turned. The ground shook like an

earthquake as the dinosaur opened its mouth and screamed into Robert's face. The sound, coming from a mouth that was big enough to chomp him up, was long and loud. *Yutyrannus* saliva streamed off the sharp teeth within its jaws, blown by its warm, foul-smelling breath. Then Riley started screaming too. Robert's ears rang as his face was covered in sticky, slimy spit.

He was scared, but the birds in the surrounding trees were even more afraid. Hundreds of them appeared, chirping in fear as they flew into the

sky – a grey and white flapping cloud.

The *yutyrannus* extended its neck, head and teeth upwards, trying to catch as many of the birds as it could between its dagger-like teeth. It caught and ate many before bounding off, following the flock across the thinly forested landscape of ancient Asia.

Once it was quiet again, Robert let out a deep breath. He peered down to see Riley looking up at him with a pale, wet face. His mouth and eyes were hanging open. 'B-b-birds?' he finally stuttered.

76

'I know!' said Robert. 'Thank goodness. I thought I was the one about to be eaten for dessert.'

Riley shook his head. 'No, I mean, what are birds doing here?'

'What do you mean? Birds aren't that rare.' Robert laughed. 'You saw a huge cassowary just today, remember?'

'I know, but I thought you said birds evolved from dinosaurs,' said Riley.

'Yes,' said Robert, 'but by the late Cretaceous period birds were already here. All kinds of animals existed together, just like in the 21st century.'

And then Robert's brain clicked. 'Oh wow, how could we not have thought of that before?' he cried.

'What?' asked Riley.

'I know where the egg is from,' said Robert, shimmying down the tree.

Riley followed him down as quickly as he could. 'Really? Where?'

Robert's feet had only touched solid ground for a second before he struggled to climb up a neighbouring tree, the one they had found the egg underneath. Until a moment ago it had been full of the large birds.

'Now where are you going?' called Riley from below.

Robert climbed fast. Soon he had found what he was looking for. Propped firmly within two prongs of a long branch was a nest. Robert climbed onto the branch and lay on it with his arms curved around its thick wood. He held the egg carefully in one hand as he shimmied towards the nest. His eyes peered over the rim of it and inside he saw a small collection of eggs. They were the same size, shape and colour as the one he had been protecting.

'Riley!' he called out. 'I found the egg's home!'

Softly, Robert placed the egg within the nest. He didn't know if a chick was growing inside, or even if the neighbouring eggs contained its brothers and sisters, but he had done the best he could. And surely sitting in a nest was better than lying on the ground all alone.

'A bird's egg!' Riley laughed, once Robert had climbed down. 'It was a simple bird's egg this whole time!'

'I know! Sometimes the easiest explanation is the right one, I guess,'

said Robert. Then he noticed something new. 'Uh, Riley, what's that behind your ear?'

'Oh,' said Riley, pulling out a long feather from the side of his face, 'I found a feather from the *yutyrannus*. I thought I'd keep it as a souvenir.'

Robert looked his friend up and down. It had been quite an adventure. They were both covered in a collection of dirt, tree bark and *yutyrannus* saliva. 'Come on,' he said, 'let's get cleaned up and find a way home!'

# CHAPTER TEN

The *segnosaurs* Robert and Riley had seen drinking from the stream when they first arrived were gone. The ancient water trickled past them, cold but refreshing. Robert and Riley splashed the chilled water all over their faces.

But it wasn't enough to budge the dirt,

so they completely dunked their grubby heads into the cold water.

Surprisingly, the water wasn't cold after all. In fact, opening his eyes, Robert could feel that the whole world had warmed up a lot.

Then there was a rustle from some bushes nearby. Riley grabbed his friend's arm. 'What's that?' he asked.

They laid low and watched. Then a creature came into view. It wasn't another dinosaur, but it was one of their ancestors: Stomp the cassowary!

'We're back,' laughed Robert.

They got up, glad to be home, and went to find the camera crew.

'You know, it's amazing how much dinosaurs and cassowaries have in common,' said Riley as they walked.

'The main similarity isn't a good one,' said Robert. 'One day those beautiful birds could be extinct too.'

Riley stroked his *yutyrannus* feather a few times before sliding it safely into his pants pocket. 'Well,' he sighed, 'at least we'll never forget them.'

'Boys! Boys! There you are,' called Simon the director, waving them over.

The crew was ready to shoot the video again. It was strange for the two friends to think that they must have only been gone a short while.

'We found Stomp the cassowary,' called Simon. 'She's a few metres behind you, pecking around within those trees. Are you ready to roll?'

Robert was tired, his head spinning with all they had just seen in Asia, 75 million years ago. But he smiled. 'Let's do this,' he said, 'before we lose that feathered tyrant again!'

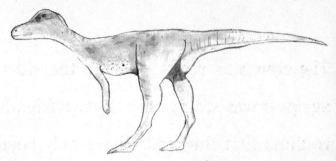

Drawn by Robert Irwin

# MICROPACHYCEPHALOSAURUS

DISCOVERED: 1978 in Shandong Province, China

ETYMOLOGY: Tiny, thick-headed lizard

PERIOD: Late Cretaceous

LENGTH: Approximately half a metre long

WEIGHT: Approximately 5 kilograms

*Micropachycephalosaurus* is the smallest of all the known pachycephalosaurs. It was bipedal and herbivorous, and currently has the longest generic name of any dinosaur.

# YUTYRANNUS

**SCIENTIFIC NAME:** Yutyrannus huali

**DISCOVERED:** 2012 in Liaoning Province, China

**ETYMOLOGY:** Beautiful feathered tyrant

**PERIOD:** Early Cretaceous

**LENGTH:** Approximately 9 metres long

**HEIGHT:** Approximately 3 metres tall

**WEIGHT:** Approximately 1.4 tonnes

Three almost complete yutyrannus skeletons have been uncovered: an adult, a sub-adult and a juvenile. The fossils were found in Liaoning Province, China, within rocks estimated to be 125 million years old.

Yutyrannus was a large, bipedal predator. A relative of the T-rex, it had relatively long arms with three fingers, and short feet. Its small horn would have added to its fearsome appearance.

Perhaps the most important feature of *yutyrannus* fossils are the visible feathers. *Yutyrannus* is currently the largest dinosaur discovered with clear, fossilised evidence of feathers. Its feathers were as long as 20 centimetres and seem to have covered its entire body. Feathers would have helped *yutyrannus* stay warm in an area with an average temperature of 10 degrees Celsius. It is possible that the feathers were also for decoration, especially the wavy feathers found on their snouts.

# FEATHERED DINOSAURS

There is now enough evidence for most scientists to believe that birds evolved from a group of theropod dinosaurs (carnivores that walked on two bird-like feet). The relationship between birds and dinosaurs was discussed as long ago as the 19th century, when the first archaeopteryx fossil was unearthed. Archaeopteryx was a primitive bird that shared many features with dinosaurs.

Scientists predicted the existence of feathered dinosaurs many years before fossils of them began appearing in the 1990s. More continue to be discovered, especially in China, and there are over 30 species of non-flying feathered dinosaurs now known.

Interestingly, feathers are not the main evidence that birds evolved from dinosaurs. From fossils we have learnt that, like birds, many dinosaurs had hollow bones, swallowed stones to help digest their food, built nests, and that they sat on their eggs to warm and protect them. We even know that many dinosaurs slept with their heads under their arms, just like you may have seen a bird sleep with their head under their wing!

Dinosaurs had feathers for a variety of reasons. Some could, perhaps, fly, but mostly they were for staying warm and looking cool to other dinosaurs!

# COLLECT THE SERIES

Interested in finding out what
Robert does when he's not
hunting dinosaurs?

Check out www.australiazoo.com.au

# Loved the book?

There's so much more
stuff to check out online